MARY ANNE AND THE
SEARCH FOR TIGGER

**Other books by
Ann M. Martin**

Rachel Parker, Kindergarten Show-off
Eleven Kids, One Summer
Ma and Pa Dracula
Yours Turly, Shirley
Ten Kids, No Pets
Slam Book
Just a Summer Romance
Missing Since Monday
With You and Without You
Me and Katie (the Pest)
Stage Fright
Inside Out
Bummer Summer

BABY-SITTERS LITTLE SISTER series
THE BABY-SITTERS CLUB mysteries
THE BABY-SITTERS CLUB series

MARY ANNE AND THE
SEARCH FOR TIGGER

Ann M. Martin

AN
APPLE
PAPERBACK

SCHOLASTIC INC.
New York Toronto London Auckland Sydney

With love to
Val,
who is also Grandma Val
and Madame Valesty

Cover art by Hodges Soileau

ISBN 0-590-67393-9

12 11 10 9 8 7 6 5 4 3   3   7 8 9/9 0 1/0

Printed in the U.S.A.   40

CHAPTER 1

"I just don't understand," Dawn Schafer said to me as we slowed down for a stop sign. "How can someone as small as Tigger knock his toys *behind* the refrigerator, so that you can't even get to them?"

I shrugged. Then I checked the street. The coast was clear, so we pedaled across the intersection. "He just does, that's all," I said. "And thank you for calling Tigger a someone instead of a something."

Dawn smiled. "I still don't get it, though."

"All I know," I said, "is that his toys roll into that space between the wall and the side of the fridge, where I ought to be able to get them out. You know where I mean?" (Dawn nodded.) "Well, they roll in there and I never see them again."

"Sort of a black hole for cat toys," said Dawn.

I giggled. "There's nothing under*neath* the

fridge. I looked there with a flashlight. That leaves in back of the fridge. And I can't get there."

"Which is why we're riding our bikes all the way downtown just to buy cat toys," said Dawn.

"Exactly," I replied.

In case you can't tell, Dawn Schafer is my friend. (I'm Mary Anne Spier.) Dawn is one of my best friends, in fact. And Tigger is my kitten. My one and only. He's a gray tiger cat with very pretty stripes. If I do say so, he's smart. Smart and pretty. And he can catch flies, which is difficult. I mean, when you only have paws.

Dawn and I were on our way to downtown Stoneybrook, Connecticut, to stock up on cat toys for Tigger, since he keeps losing them behind the fridge. His favorites are those plastic balls with a little bell inside. They come three in a pack, and he loses about three a week, so cat toys can be expensive to me. Thank goodness I earn lots of money baby-sitting.

Dawn and I stopped at a traffic light. We had reached Stoneybrook's main street (which is about as small as Stoneybrook is), and were only three blocks from the pet store.

"Hey, what did your dad say about the date last night?" asked Dawn.

We laughed. Dawn's mom and my dad go out sometimes. We really wish they would get married, but we can't help laughing. It's just so weird to see your own parents *dating*. Especially dating each other. They go out with other people, too, but when Dawn's mom has a date with my dad, she puts on all this makeup and checks her clothes twenty times and then asks Dawn to check her clothes again. And my dad puts on after-shave that smells like the dentist's office and gets nervous and can barely speak to me. Then they go somewhere together. What a pair.

By the way, the reason they can date is Dawn's parents are divorced and my mom died ages ago. I really don't even remember her.

"I think my dad had fun when they went out," I told Dawn. "What about your mom?"

"Same," she replied. Then she announced, "Pet store," and stopped her bike. "Hey, I just thought of something." Dawn was grinning.

"What?" I asked.

"Well," she replied, "there's not much space behind your refrigerator, right?"

"Right." We were chaining our bikes to a lamppost.

"Probably just enough space for the width of one toy, right?"

"Right."

"So Tigger's toys are probably behind the fridge in a line. And when the line reaches the wall, there won't be room for any more toys, right?"

"Right," I replied as we entered the store.

"And *then* Tigger's toys can't get lost and you won't have to keep buying new ones."

"Yeah!" Honestly, Dawn is so logical.

I headed for the cat toy department and picked up two packages of Tigger's toys. In one package, the balls were half pink and half green. In the other, they were half orange and half yellow. I like to give Tigger a little variety in his toys. Then I began looking over the cat treats. Maybe I should buy some fancy food for Tigger.

I was counting my money when Dawn tapped me on the arm. "We better go," she said. "Club meeting in forty-five minutes."

"Okay. Just let me buy these." I held up the toys.

I stood in line at the counter, thinking about the Baby-sitters Club. My closest friends are all in the club: Kristy Thomas (she's my other best friend), Claudia Kishi, Jessi Ramsey, Mallory Pike, Dawn, and Logan Bruno (an associate member, who doesn't usually attend club meetings. I'll explain that later.) Logan is basically my boyfriend, and he is incredible in every way. He's incredible-looking and incredibly nice and incredibly thoughtful and, well, incredibly incredible.

(There is also one person who's in the club who is not a close friend, and one person who is a close friend who's not really in the club anymore. I'll tell you about them later.)

The Baby-sitters Club is more a business than a club. My friends and I sit for families in our neighborhoods. We get a lot of jobs and earn a lot of money. And I spend a lot of my money right here in the pet store. The club was started by Kristy Thomas, our president. (I'm the secretary, by the way.) In some ways, Kristy is like me, but in more ways, she's my exact opposite. I think that's why she was my very first best friend. That and the fact that we lived next door to each other from the time we were born. Here are the things that are the same about us: We're small for our age and have brown hair and brown eyes. Here are the ways in which we're different: I'm shy and sort of held in; Kristy is outgoing and can be a loudmouth. I'm beginning to take an interest in what I wear; Kristy couldn't care less. She always wears jeans, a turtleneck, a sweater, and running shoes. (Well, not in the summer, of course, but you know what I mean.)

Kristy has more ideas than anyone I know. She's always thinking of things to do, or finding ways to solve problems. You can almost *see* her brain at work. Lately, Kristy's life hasn't been too easy, though. It hasn't been bad, just not easy. For the longest time, she lived with her mom, her three brothers, and her collie, Louie, right next door to me. (Her parents had gotten a divorce.) Then her mom met this millionaire, Watson Brewer, and the next thing I knew, they'd decided to get married. After the wedding, Kristy's family moved across town into Watson's mansion. There was more room in the mansion, of course, but Kristy was upset. She had left her old neighborhood and her friends behind. And then Louie the collie died, which was terribly sad. On the other hand, Kristy gained a new little step-brother and stepsister, whom she loves very much, and her family had gotten an adorable puppy. . . . And *then* they adopted a two-year-old girl! Kristy's life is never dull.

The vice-president of the Baby-sitters Club is Claudia Kishi. What a difference from Kristy and me. Claud, who lives across the street from Kristy's old house, is absolutely beautiful. Sophisticated, too. She's Japanese-American, and her eyes are dark and beautifully almond-shaped. Her hair is long and black and she wears it all different ways. And her complexion is perfect. It's her clothes that amaze me though. (I think they amaze everyone.) Claud mixes and matches the weirdest stuff and comes up with the coolest outfits. Like a loose blouse with a fake coat of arms on it worn over a very short black skirt. Around her waist, a scarf. On her feet, short black boots. Dangling from her ears, dinosaurs. And her hair might be piled on top of her head and held in place with hairpins that look like seahorses. She combines all this stuff — and she looks fantastic.

Claud's hobbies are reading Nancy Drew mysteries, eating junk food, and especially working at her art. She's really talented and takes lots of classes. She's good at drawing, painting, pottery, you name it. Unfortunately, as far as her parents are concerned, Claud's art does not make up for the fact that she's smart but a poor student. After all, her older sister, Janine, is an actual genius. Luckily for Claudia, her grandmother Mimi lives with their family, and she and Claud are very close, even now when I can see that Mimi's mind is starting to wander and get sort of fuzzy.

Dawn is our club's treasurer, and you already know a little about her, but I'll fill you in on the rest. Dawn hasn't been living in Stoneybrook for long. She grew up in California with her parents and her younger brother, Jeff. But her parents split up, and Mrs. Schafer brought Dawn and Jeff to Stoneybrook to live, leaving Mr. Schafer three thousand miles behind. Dawn's mom chose Stoneybrook because she grew up here, and that's how she and my father know each other — they went to high school together years and years ago. Anyway, Dawn likes Connecticut okay, but Jeff never did. He always missed California and his dad. So after awhile he moved back. That was hard on Dawn. Now her family is split in half. But Dawn is very practical. She takes things as they come. She's not laid-back, exactly, she's just a real individual. Dawn solves her own problems and makes her own decisions in her own ways. And she practically runs the old farmhouse she and her mom live in. That's because her mom is totally scatterbrained. Nice, but living on some other planet. I wonder what kind of stepmother she would make.

Dawn has the longest, palest blonde hair you'll ever see, and bright blue eyes. She looks as Californian as all the health food she eats. (Dawn would never touch the junk food Claud loves.) I am *so* glad Dawn moved here because she's a great best friend. And it's neat that our parents are dating.

Jessi Ramsey and Mallory Pike are the junior officers of the Baby-sitters Club. That's because they're the youngest in the club. Jessi and Mal are eleven and in sixth grade at Stoneybrook Middle School, and the rest of us are thirteen and in eighth grade at SMS. Like Kristy and me, Jessi and Mal are best friends who are somewhat alike and somewhat different. Unlike Kristy and me, I think they're more alike than different. Let me describe the two of them for you, and you can make your own decision. I'll start with Jessi.

I might as well be straightforward (even though I hardly ever am), and say right out that Jessi's family is black. They moved to Stoneybrook near the beginning of the school year, and they're one of the few black families here. A lot of people gave them a hard time at first, but things have gotten better. Jessi is a ballet dancer, a good one (I've seen her perform), and she *looks* like a dancer. She pulls her hair back from her face into a knot above her neck, and she has lo-o-o-ong legs. Besides dancing, Jessi likes reading. (She has to wear glasses for that.)

Jessi is very close to her family. She lives with her parents, her younger sister, Becca, her baby brother, Squirt, and a pet hamster. She feels like she doesn't quite fit in at school, and she thinks her parents sometimes treat her like a baby. But mostly she's happy, especially since she met Mallory.

Now Mallory may be white, and she may have seven brothers and sisters (plus two parents and a hamster), *but* she wears glasses, she *loves* to read, and also to write and draw (she might want to write books for children one day), and she also feels that she doesn't always fit in at school, and especially that her parents sometimes treat her like a baby. The Pikes and the Ramseys did give in a little while ago and let Mal and Jessi get their ears pierced, but both of them still wish for trendier clothes. You can see how much Mal and Jessi have in common.

I guess that's about it. Logan's in the club, too, but I've already told you about him. He's the incredibly incredible one, remember? Then there's Shannon Kilbourne, whom I don't know very well (she's another associate member, like Logan, who doesn't go to our meetings), and Stacey McGill, who used to be in the club, but who moved away. More about them and everyone else later. Honest.

"Here's your change, miss," said the man behind the counter of the pet store. He handed me seventy-three cents and the bag full of cat toys.

"Thanks," I replied. (I hate being called "miss.")

Dawn and I headed out of the store. On the way, I passed the flea-and-tick products.

"Hmm," I said, stopping, "I wonder if Tigger needs a bottle of Doctor Herkie's Flea Tonic."

"How bad are his fleas?" asked Dawn.

"He doesn't have any yet," I replied.

Dawn pulled me out of the store. We unchained our bikes and began to ride home.

"Dawn?" I said when we were about halfway there. (Actually I shouted it. She was riding in front of me and the wind was blowing against us.)

"What?"

"Can we go to my house before the meeting? I want to give Tigger his toys. We'll have time." I also wanted to get the mail. It is my absolute favorite thing to do. I don't know why. There's hardly ever anything for me.

"Sure," Dawn called back.

So we stopped at my mailbox. Sure enough, nothing for me. But some days there are surprises. You never know. We parked our bikes near the front walk and ran inside, where I opened Tigger's packages of toys for him. Then we ran back out and across the street to Claudia's house. It was time for the Wednesday afternoon meeting of the Baby-sitters Club.

CHAPTER 2

Dawn and I were not the first to arrive at the meeting of the Baby-sitters Club, but we weren't the last, either. Kristy Thomas and Claudia Kishi were already there.

Kristy was sitting in her official presidential position — bolt upright in Claud's director's chair, wearing her visor, a pencil stuck over one ear. She was looking through our club notebook.

Claudia was doing something we've seen her do a thousand times before. She was lying on her stomach, half under the bed, rooting around in the stuff stored there. She was probably rooting for one of two things — art supplies or junk food. See, Claud's room is sort of a . . . . Well, I'm sorry, but "rat hole" is the best word I can come up with. Okay, it isn't *that* bad, but it is messy. Claudia needs all sorts of supplies for her projects, and there just isn't enough room for them on her shelves and in her closet. So she's stored boxes of stuff under her bed, in stacks against the wall, everywhere. She's also a junk-food addict, and she really has to hide her Fritos and Doritos and Heath Bars and M&Ms well. That's because her parents don't approve of her habit and told Claud, "No junk food," but she just couldn't give it up. It's hidden everywhere — in the boxes of art supplies, in drawers, even in her pillow.

So Dawn and I weren't too surprised to see Claudia half under the bed. I'm not supposed to eat right before dinner. Even so, I hoped she was searching for food, not art materials. I was pretty hungry.

"Hi, you guys," said Kristy with a smile, as Dawn and I entered Claud's room. "What's going on?"

(We had all just seen each other at school, but that didn't matter. Every time we get together, it's as if we haven't spoken in a week.)

"We rode downtown to buy toys for Tigger," I replied. "What's Claud doing?"

"Looking for my Double Stuf Oreos," answered Claudia from under the bed, only it sounded as if she said, "Lummy fummy dummy fuff ooeey."

"Oh, *good!*" exclaimed Kristy. "Double Stuf Oreos."

"How on earth could you understand her?" Dawn asked Kristy as she and I settled ourselves gingerly on the bed. We didn't want to crush the vice-president beneath us.

Kristy shrugged. "Practice."

Claudia emerged from her junk-food hiding place with an unopened package of Double Stuf Oreos in one hand.

"Oh, yum," said Kristy, looking as if she might faint from happiness.

While Claud was opening the cookies, Jessi and Mal arrived.

"Great. We're all here," announced Kristy. "Let's begin."

Mal and Jessi took their usual places on the floor, Claudia passed the cookies around, and Kristy called our meeting to order. As president, that's one of her jobs.

Maybe I better tell you a little about the club and how it works. We hold meetings three times a week, every Monday, Wednesday, and Friday afternoon from five-thirty until six. Our clients call us during those times to say that they need sitters, and then we schedule the jobs for ourselves, depending on who's free.

How do parents know when to call us? Well, I'll go back to the beginning and tell you how

14

the club started. Then you can find out for yourself.

Kristy is the one who thought up the Baby-sitters Club. (That's the main reason she's the president.) See, way back at the start of seventh grade, Kristy and her family were still living next door to me and across the street from Claud. Kristy's little brother, David Michael, was six then, and Kristy and her two older brothers, Sam and Charlie (they're in high school), were responsible for baby-sitting for him most of the time, since Mrs. Thomas (well, now she's Mrs. Brewer) has a full-time job. But the day came when Kristy's mom needed a sitter for one particular afternoon, and no-body — not Kristy, not Sam, not Charlie — was free. So she got on the phone and began making call after call, in search of a sitter. That was when Kristy got her great idea. What a waste of time, she thought, for her mom to have to make so many calls. Wouldn't it be easy if she could make one call and reach several sitters? Surely one of them would be free.

That was it! Kristy would get together with several of her friends, we would meet a few times a week, and when someone called, one of us was bound to be free for a job. So the caller was practically guaranteed a sitter. Kristy asked Claudia and me to be in her club. When we decided we needed one more member, Claud introduced us to Stacey McGill, a new friend of hers. Stacey and her parents had just moved to Stoneybrook from New York City. We liked Stacey right away and asked her to join. Then we did some advertising so people would know about our sitting service and how to reach us. And soon we were in business. Kristy, Claudia, Stacey, and I became the first president, vice-president, treasurer, and secretary of the Baby-sitters Club.

By the time Dawn moved here, we were doing so much business that we wanted her in the club, too, and when Stacey had to move back to New York, we replaced her with both Jessi and Mal. So our club has grown to six people. Actually, it's seven people as far as I'm concerned. Stacey isn't really gone; she's just the New York branch of the Baby-sitters Club!

Kristy runs the club in a very businesslike manner. She insists that's the only way to do things. And so we keep a club record book and a club notebook. The record book is *really* important. It's full of information. As secretary, it's my job to keep track of our clients' names and addresses and stuff like that, and also to schedule all of our sitting jobs on the appointment pages. And Dawn, as treasurer, keeps track of our money in the record book, too.

The notebook is something that most of us don't like too much. In the notebook, we have to write up every single job we go on. Then we're responsible for reading the notebook once a week to see what's happened when our friends were sitting. I have to admit that finding out how other people handle sitting problems is helpful . . . but, boy, do we get tired of writing in that book.

It was one of Kristy's ideas, though, and that's another reason she's president. She's always coming up with new projects or ideas to keep the club fresh. For instance, Kristy dreamed up Kid-Kits. Kid-Kits are decorated boxes filled with games and toys and books — mostly our old things. Each of us has made a Kid-Kit. Whenever I take mine on a sitting job, the kids are thrilled. For some reason, another person's toys are always more interesting than your own. So the kids are happy and their parents are happy, and when parents are happy, they call our club again! Kid-Kits are good for business.

As vice-president, Claud's job is . . . well, she doesn't exactly have a job. She's the vice-president because she has her very own phone and private phone number, so her room is a good place for us to hold our meetings. We don't have to tie up anyone's line three times a week. Claud is really nice about letting us use her things and eat her junk food.

You already know what my job is about. I keep records and schedule sitting jobs. In order to do that, I have to know when Claud's art lessons are, Jessi's ballet classes, Mal's orthodontist appointments (she just got braces), and that sort of thing. Sometimes I complain about my job, but mostly I like it.

Dawn took over the office of treasurer when Stacey moved away. Her job is to collect dues money from us club members every Monday and to make sure we always have enough money in our treasury. We use the treasury money to buy new things for the Kid-Kits (crayons, coloring books, anything that gets used up), to pay Kristy's brother Charlie to drive her to and from meetings now that she lives on the other side of town, and to treat ourselves to a sleepover or a party every now and then.

Our junior officers, Jessi and Mallory, don't have actual jobs. "Junior" means that since they're younger than the rest of us, they aren't allowed to sit at night, unless they're sitting for their own brothers and sisters. They're a big help, though. They take a lot of the afternoon jobs, which frees us older club members to take the evening jobs.

Last but certainly not least, there are Logan and Shannon. Logan and Shannon are associate members. That means that they don't come to meetings, but we can call on them if a job comes up that none of the rest of us is free to take. Believe it or not, this happens. And we'd hate to have to tell one of our clients that we couldn't provide her (or him) with a sitter. Shannon Kilbourne, by the way, is a friend of Kristy's. She lives across the street from her in Kristy's new neighborhood.

On the day I went toy-shopping for Tigger, Kristy had just barely called the meeting to order when the phone rang.

We looked at each other and smiled. A job call so early in a meeting must be a good sign.

Claudia reached for the phone, a plastic charm bracelet dangling from her wrist. "Hello, Baby-sitters Club," she said. There was a pause. Then she put her hand over the receiver. "Oh, Mary A-anne," she called to me in a singsong voice, "it's for you-ou."

I took the phone, glancing at Kristy. She doesn't like us to get personal calls during meetings.

"Hello?" I said.

"Hi!" replied a cheerful voice.

Logan! I was really happy to hear from him. I just hoped he was calling about business.

"What's up?" I asked him.

"I need a sitter." Actually, he said, "Ah need a sittuh." (Logan's family moved here from Louisville, Kentucky, not long ago.)

"For Kerry and Hunter?" I asked. Kerry is Logan's nine-year-old sister and Hunter is his five-year-old brother. None of us has baby-sat for them before, because Logan always does it.

"Yeah. It's for this Saturday afternoon. Mom and Dad have some tennis thing lined up with friends of theirs, and I'm going to baseball practice at school. I was supposed to sit, but then practice came up. Can one of you do it?"

I was dying to do it, of course, but I had to treat this job like any other. "I'll check our schedules and call you back in just a few minutes, okay?"

"Okay."

This is how we handle club jobs. The person who gets the phone call or who answers the phone never just takes a job. It's open for everyone.

I told the others about the job as I looked at the appointment pages in the record book. "Well," I said, "Kristy, you and Mallory and I are free."

My friends were *very* generous and let me take the job. I called Logan back. "What's all that sneezing I hear?" I asked, after I'd told him that I would be the sitter.

"Oh, it's my brother. It's allergy season."

"Poor Hunter," I replied, remembering his bare, dust-free bedroom. "He — " I stopped. I had glanced at Kristy. Her eyeballs were practically falling out of her head in her effort to get me to end my personal conversation.

So I said good-bye quickly. Our meeting continued. When it was over, I dashed out the door, calling good-bye to Claudia's grandmother Mimi, who replied in confusion, "I will take six, please."

Then I ran home to play with Tigger.

CHAPTER 3

My dad used to be strict with me. Very strict. It wasn't so long ago that I had to fix my hair in braids and wear clothes he picked out, that I had to live in a little-girl room, wasn't allowed to ride my bicycle downtown, couldn't talk on the phone after dinner unless it was about homework, etc. I think my dad made up those rules because he was trying to be a good mother. That may sound funny, but I'm pretty sure it's true. He was nervous about raising a daughter by himself and he wanted me to turn out okay, so he decided he had to practically take over my life.

Luckily, he and I have both been changing lately. I've shown him that I'm more grown up and mature than he thought, and he realized that he doesn't have to live my life for me. So he let me take my hair out of braids and fix up my room so it isn't so babyish. Then came bigger changes. Now I can go places with my

22

friends and talk on the phone after dinner. But Dad is still Dad. There's a ten-minute time limit on phone calls. And if Logan comes over when Dad isn't home, Logan has to stay outside. He is not allowed in.

Which is why the two of us were sitting outside one Friday afternoon that was so gray it was almost raining. But we had no choice. Well, I suppose we *could* have gone inside. How would Dad have known? But I just am not able to break one of his rules. I'm afraid he'll find out somehow. Magically, maybe. Anyway, a rule is a rule.

Besides, it *wasn't* raining, and it was fairly warm, so being outside wasn't actually unpleasant. How could it be unpleasant with Logan next to me, and Tigger playing at our feet?

Logan had untied one of his sneakers and was dangling the lace in front of Tigger. Tigger thought this was a great game. He batted at the lace. He tried to catch it. He stood on his hind legs and stretched out his round tummy, reaching as far as he could.

"Aw, look. He's so cute!" I said. (I say that, oh, sixty-five times a day.)

Logan grinned. I had said it ten or twelve times just since he'd come over.

I changed the subject. "I'm glad today is

Friday. I like school and everything, but . . ."

"But there's nothing like two days off," supplied Logan.

"Right."

"And think of it. This happens once a week. Boy, are we lucky. I'd like to thank whoever arranged things that way."

Tigger got tired of playing with the lace then and darted away from us. He pounced on a bug. He ran after a seed pod that dropped from a tree.

"Aw, he's so cute," I said. Then I called, "Careful, Tigger!" Tigger has only been allowed outdoors for a couple of weeks now. Sometimes I even let him go out alone. He can stay happily in the yard for hours — playing and napping. I worry about him, being outside on his own. Then I remember how great it felt when Dad finally let go of me. I wonder — does Dad worry about me every day the way I worry about Tigger?

"You're sure quiet," said Logan suddenly.

I looked over at him. "I was thinking about how Dad treats me and how I treat Tigger and — "

"Again?" said Logan sharply.

I paused. Logan hardly ever speaks like that. I decided to ignore it. "How's baseball practice going?"

24

"Fine."

"How's the coach? What's his name?"

"Coach Blake."

Conversational dead end. Okay. . . . Now what?

"Hi-hi!" called a little voice.

It could only belong to Jamie Newton. I glanced up and there he was, standing at the edge of our yard.

"Hi!" I called back.

Jamie's family lives nearby, so the members of the Baby-sitters Club, especially Claudia, sit for the Newtons all the time. Jamie is four and has a baby sister named Lucy.

Jamie ran across the lawn. "Oh, goody!" he exclaimed. "There's Tigger."

Tigger looked like he might be tiring out. He was sitting in the grass — very neatly, with his tail curled around his front feet. But he wasn't doing anything. Nothing I knew about, anyway. Maybe he was doing some secret cat thing.

"Can I play with Tigger, Mary Anne? Please?" asked Jamie.

"Sure," I answered, "but carefully. I'm not sure he wants to play right now."

Jamie lay on the ground near Tigger. He and Tigger looked at each other.

I glanced at Logan. Usually Logan and I

25

would have turned to each other at a moment like that and smiled. But Logan was staring into the distance.

"Earth to Logan, Earth to Logan," I said, cupping my hands around my mouth. "Come in, Logan."

"I *am* in, Mary Anne," he replied, without bothering to look at me.

I felt stung.

In the grass, Jamie inched closer to my kitten. "Tigger, Tigger, Tigger, Tigger, Tigger," he whispered. He swept one hand from side to side.

Tigger immediately fell into a crouch position. His head moved back and forth, following Jamie's hand. Suddenly — POUNCE! Tigger landed on Jamie's hand. (Luckily Tigger's little claws are only about as sharp as pine needles.)

Jamie burst into giggles. "Tigger!" he squealed. He rolled onto his back and put Tigger on his tummy.

I glanced at Logan again. This time at least he was smiling. "Pretty cute," I commented.

"Boy," said Jamie, "I sure do wish I had a pet. I'd get a . . . dog. No, a rabbit. No, a — a chicken. No, a cat. I mean, a kitten. That's it. I'd get a kitten just like Tigger. Gray and white. And pounsive."

"Pounsive?" said Logan and I at the same

26

time. I elbowed Logan as a way of telling him not to laugh. He didn't.

"Hi, Jamie!"

"Hi, Jamie!"

"Hi, Myriah! Hi, Gabbie! Hi-hi!" called Jamie. Standing in their yard next door were Myriah and Gabbie Perkins. The girls are good friends of Jamie's.

The Perkins family moved into Kristy's house when Kristy and her mom and brothers moved to Watson's. Considering I lost my best friend then, I feel lucky that such a nice family moved in. Us club members baby-sit at the Perkinses' a lot. Myriah is five and a half, Gabbie is two and a half, and their little sister Laura is an infant.

"Come on over!" Jamie called to the girls.

"Overrun with kids," I thought I heard Logan murmur, but I wasn't sure.

"No, come over here!" cried Gabbie. "Come on, Jamie. We have something to show you."

"Okay." Jamie set Tigger on the ground. He called good-bye to us, and ran next door.

"Want something to drink?" I asked Logan.

"Sure," he replied.

I knew exactly what he wanted. That's how well we know each other. I didn't even need to ask him.

"Be right back," I said, as I got to my feet.

Logan didn't like having to wait outside (I could tell by the look on his face), but what could we do? I ran inside, opened two sodas, and ran back outside. I handed one to Logan as I sat down again.

"So," I said, as I settled myself on the stoop, "how are Kerry and Hunter?"

"You mean, what are you getting yourself into when you sit tomorrow?"

"No!" I said, even though I knew Logan was teasing me.

Logan smiled. "Well, Hunter's allergies are as bad as ever, and Kerry is going through a stage."

"A stage?"

"Yeah. She's been saying that we treat her like a baby. I think she wants to be, you know, more independent. She could also use a few friends. She hasn't really made any since we moved here."

I nodded, staring down the street.

A few moments later I said, "I think we have more company." Charlotte Johanssen was headed our way. She's eight, another kid our club sits for. And she reminds me of myself — nice, but shy, trying hard to please people.

"Hi!" I called to Charlotte as she reached the end of our driveway. "Want to come see

Tigger?" I turned to Logan and whispered, "It's all right with you, isn't it?"

"Oh, sure."

I couldn't tell what sort of tone was in Logan's voice, but I didn't worry about it. I watched Charlotte approach Tigger. Now he was a little livelier. He waited until Charlotte had almost reached him, then he jumped away.

Charlotte began to giggle. She sat down in the grass. She closed her eyes. "Oh, I can't see you, Mr. Tigger," she sang. "So come back to me. Come on back."

Charlotte sat very still, peeking every now and then. Tigger crept toward her, right into her lap.

"Gotcha!" exclaimed Charlotte, opening her eyes and cupping him in her hands.

Logan laughed. So did Charlotte and I. ("Oh, he's so cute," I said.) Tigger looked at the three of us with surprised eyes. What had happened?

"Gosh," said Charlotte, as she turned Tigger onto his back, "if I could have three wishes, you know what I'd wish for?"

"What?" Logan and I asked at the same time.

"Tigger," she replied. "A pet of my own."

"And the other two wishes?" asked Logan.

"Tigger and Tigger."

The three of us laughed — and I watched Logan and remembered something. I remembered one reason I had liked him so much when I was first getting to know him. Well, I have to admit, when I first saw him, I just thought he was gorgeous. But later I liked a lot of other things about him. For instance, he's good with kids. And he can laugh easily. (Obviously today was not one of his better days. But laughing just now had reminded me of that.)

You know what I still can't figure out, though? I can't figure out why Logan likes me. Why would any boy like shy me better than so-phisticated, outgoing Claudia? Or self-assured Dawn?

I didn't know then and I still don't know now. But Logan put his arm around me, and we watched Charlotte and Tigger for a long time. At that moment, it didn't seem to matter why Logan likes me.

At last Charlotte stood up. "I better go," she said.

Beside me, Logan stood up, too. "Same here." (I think he was getting cold. I was.)

I sighed. "Okay."

Charlotte ran off, and Logan jumped on his ten-speed and pedaled away.

I scooped up Tigger. "Come on, Bigger

Tigger," I said. "Time to go inside. I have a meeting of the Baby-sitters Club and you've been outdoors long enough."

But Tigger struggled and mewed. He did not want to leave the yard. So finally I let him stay outside. As I ran across the street to Claudia's house, I could see him pouncing on invisible things in the grass.

CHAPTER 4

"Hi, Tigger, wherever you are!" I called. "Come see me!"

Our meeting was over and I was at home again. It was time to start dinner. Dad and I like to eat pretty soon after he returns from work, and he returns between six and six-thirty most nights. So as soon as I'm home from club meetings, I get busy.

That night I set a huge pot of water on the stove. At breakfast that morning, Dad and I had decided we wanted spaghetti for dinner. And with that, I thought, a salad and some garlic bread. I'm not much of a cook, but I can throw a meal together.

I was busy getting vegetables out of the refrigerator when I realized something. Tigger wasn't running between my feet like he usually does at this hour of the day. I always feed him while I'm making dinner — and he knows it.

Where was he? He hadn't come when I'd

called. I checked to make sure that his special cat door was open. Sure enough, it was. I was surprised that he hadn't come inside while I was at Claudia's. He knew it was getting to be dinnertime . . . didn't he?

Well, wait a second. Maybe he *was* inside. He has an awful lot of good hiding places.

"Tigger, Tigger, Tigger!" I called as I got his food out.

I chose a can of King Kat Liver 'n' Beef. I spooned a quarter of it into his bowl. Then I poured in a little milk and stirred it up. Can you believe it? Milk actually isn't very good for cats, especially male cats, but it isn't bad for kittens. And Tigger is so little that I need to mix the grown-up cat food with something to make it mushier.

I set his dish on his place mat, his special cat mat that says FOOD PLEASE. Then I called him again.

No Tigger.

"I know you're hiding," I said loudly. "Aren't you hungry?"

No Tigger.

"All right. I'll just have to look for you."

In our house are a million places where a kitten could hide. There are also several where a kitten could get stuck. Twice, Tigger has been snoozing in the laundry room when the doors somehow swung closed on him. I marched to the laundry room. The doors were closed! Goody.

"Tigger!" I called.

I opened the door. No Tigger.

Sometimes he climbs onto a high place, such as the mantelpiece over the fireplace, and then can't get down. I checked the mantelpiece. No Tigger.

Okay. It was time for a room-by-room search. In a room-by-room search, I look through each room thoroughly. If I don't find Tigger in one room, I close the door to the room (if it has a door) and go on to the next one.

I began upstairs. I searched the bedrooms and the bathrooms. I didn't see Tigger, so I closed the door at the head of the stairs and ran down to the first floor.

I was on my hands and knees looking under a chair when I heard my father calling me.

"I'm here, Dad!" I replied. "In the living room."

I backed away from the chair and stood up.

"What's going on?" asked my father. He crossed the room and gave me a kiss. "There's water on the stove but the burner isn't on, and there are vegetables all over the table. It looks as if you stopped in the middle of making dinner."

"Sorry. I guess I did. I can't find Tigger. And I've looked everywhere for him. Well, everywhere inside. He's never missed dinner."

"I guess we better search for him outside then," said Dad.

I gave Dad a grateful look. "Right now? That would be terrific."

"I'll go get the torches."

The torches are these gigantic flashlights we have. Each is bright enough to light up New York City.

I put a jacket on and Dad found the torches. He handed one to me and we went outside.

"Ti-i-i-igger! Ti-i-i-igger!" we called. We walked all around our yard. We shone the lights under bushes, up trees, in shrubbery. The longer we looked, the worse I felt. There was this awful feeling in the pit of my stomach, like I had swallowed a pebble and it had grown into a rock. Now it was growing into a boulder.

Dad must have seen me looking discouraged, because he said brightly, "I've got an idea," and ran inside. When he came out, he was carrying two of Tigger's toys. He gave me one, and we walked around the yard again, this time shaking the toys so that the balls jingled.

"Come play! Ti-i-i-igger, come play!"

No Tigger. (The rock had just about reached boulder proportions.)

"Dad!" I called, and he came running around the side of the house. "I don't think he's here. I really don't."

My father put his arm around my shoulders. "Maybe not. Maybe he's off on an adventure. Anyway, I don't think there's any point in looking for him outside now. It's too dark. Besides, if he were around here, he would have come to us by now."

I nodded. "I know."

"So let's go in."

Dad and I went into a house. A huge lump was forming in my throat. Maybe it was that boulder.

"I suggest we go on and make ourselves a nice dinner," my father said cheerfully. "If Tigger's off enjoying himself, then we might as well enjoy ourselves."

I looked at Tigger's bowl. The food was starting to congeal and the milk was turning brown. Tigger probably wouldn't eat it tonight. How sad.

Dad saw me looking at the dish and said, "When I was growing up, our next-door neighbors had a cat who disappeared at least once a week. He just liked to take trips."

"But Tigger is so little," I replied. I turned on the burner under the pot of water, while Dad began cutting up the tomatoes and cu-

cumbers and celery and carrots for our salad. He didn't look worried. How come I felt so worried? Because I'm a worrywart, that's why.

We ate our dinner. Well, Dad ate his dinner. I tried to eat mine, but all I could get down were three mouthfuls of salad.

"Mary Anne," said my father, looking at my full plate, "what time is it?"

"Seven-thirty?" I answered. (Why was he asking? He was wearing his watch.)

"And when was the last time you saw Tigger?"

"Just before five-thirty."

"So he's only been missing for two hours," Dad pointed out. "He could be taking a nap somewhere, for all we know."

"He did have a pretty exciting afternoon," I said slowly. "Lots of visitors. And he does sleep soundly."

"I'll say," said Dad. "He could sleep through a tornado."

I felt cheered up. I felt so cheered up that I called Dawn and said, "You'll never guess what. Tigger is off taking a nap, and he's hidden himself so well that Dad and I can't find him!"

Dawn giggled. She likes Tigger stories. Then she said, "Okay, my turn. *You'll* never guess what. Our parents are going out again."

"They are? Dad didn't say anything."

"Well, it's no big deal. They're just going to a parents meeting at school together. But that's something, isn't it?"

"Sure," I replied. "That's something."

Dawn and I talked for the exact ten minutes that I'm allowed. Then we hung up. Then she called back. We talked for ten more minutes. That's one way of getting around Dad's telephone rule without actually breaking it.

After the second call, we hung up for good, though. I didn't want to press my luck. I watched some TV. I read two chapters in this really great book called *A Swiftly Tilting Planet*, by Madeleine L'Engle. I checked over my list of weekend homework assignments. And then I looked at my watch. Ten o'clock! Not only was it almost time to go to bed, but Tigger had been missing for four and a half hours.

I marched into my father's den, where he was doing some paperwork.

"Excuse me," I said, "but do you think Tigger has been taking a four-and-a-half hour nap?"

"Hmm?" Dad looked bleary-eyed.

"It's ten o'clock. Do you know where Tigger is?" I said.

Dad didn't get the joke, but he did look vaguely surprised. "Still missing, is he? Mary

Anne, he'll turn up. He's just gone off on a jaunt. Cats do that, you know."

I wasn't convinced, but I went to bed anyway. I left my window open in case he turned up outside and began mewing. Then I lay down in bed. But I couldn't go to sleep. How could I sleep with Tigger missing? And he *was* missing, just like Dad had said.

He had disappeared.

At eleven-thirty, my father went to bed. I know because I was still awake. I knelt on my bed and looked out the window. I couldn't see anything, though. The sky was still overcast, so the clouds covered the moon.

I lay down again. At last I went to sleep. I woke up at one-thirty, thinking I heard mewing.

"Tigger? Tigger?" I called softly.

Nothing. I must have dreamed it.

The same thing happened at ten minutes past three, at 4:45, at 6:20, and at seven-thirty, when I finally decided to get up.

I ran down to the kitchen. "Is Tigger back?" I asked my father. He was sitting at the table with a cup of coffee and the newspaper.

This time he looked more worried than surprised. "No," said Dad. "He's not."

I sank into my chair. Now what?

Dad had fixed pancakes for breakfast and I tried to eat them, but I couldn't. Instead, I excused myself from the table, went to my room, got dressed, then went out to search the yard. The clouds were gone and the day was sunny and bright, but I couldn't find Tigger. I was glad there were no bodies in the road or under high trees, but . . . where *was* he?

All morning, I watched for Tigger and worried. When afternoon came, I realized I would have to leave for Logan's to baby-sit. It was the last thing I wanted to do. But Dad would be home. He could watch for Tigger. And with any luck, by the time I got back, Tigger would be back, too.

CHAPTER 5

"Ah-choo! Ah-choo! . . . AH-CHOO!"

Sneezing was the first sound I heard when Kerry opened the door for me at the Brunos' house.

"Hi, Kerry," I said. I was trying as hard as I possibly could to act normal. "Is that Hunter I hear?"

Kerry nodded. She closed the door behind me. "Poor Hunter. All he does is sneeze."

"Where's Logan?" I asked. I was sort of hoping to be able to tell him about Tigger before he left for practice. Until now, I hadn't felt like talking about it with any of my friends.

"Oh, Logan's gone already. And, boy, was he in a grouchy mood," said Kerry, as she led me into the living room. "He hardly talked to any of us."

"Yeah, he just growled," added a stuffy voice. "Like this. Grrr. Grrr."

I smiled. "Hi, Hunter."

"Hi," he replied.

I knew Kerry and Hunter pretty well even though I'd never baby-sat for them. I'd just spent a lot of time at their house. And I'd have been looking forward to sitting for them, but now because of Tigger, I was mostly just worrying.

Hunter dragged himself into the living room, sat down on the couch, and sneezed. Kerry handed him a tissue.

"Thack you," he said. "There bust be sub dust id here."

I smiled. Kerry and Hunter are a neat brother and sister. They don't look a thing alike, but they get along great. Kerry looks like Logan. She has his eyes and nose, but unlike her big brother, her hair is very blonde, thick, and straight. Hunter, on the hand, has the same dark-blonde, curly hair as his brother — but his face is completely different. He looks more like his father, while Logan and Kerry look more like their mother.

I was thinking about that when Mr. and Mrs. Bruno came into the living room, wearing their tennis clothes.

"Hello, Mary Anne," they greeted me.

Mrs. Bruno bent down to look at Hunter. "Oh." She clucked her tongue. "Now your eyes look bad, too."

"They're rudding," said Hunter pitifully. "They itch."

Mrs. Bruno shook her head.

"Is there anything special I should do for Hunter?" I asked Logan's mother.

"Nope," she replied. "Just the usual. He better stay indoors today. His bedroom would be the best place for him, but I don't want to coop him up in there. *Don't* let him near Logan's room, though. It's a mess."

"A dust factory," added Kerry.

"And he's got down pillows," finished up Mrs. Bruno.

"Is there anything I should give Hunter?" I asked. "Does he have allergy pills?"

"Yes, but he just took them. He'll be all right, won't you, pumpkin?" said Mrs. Bruno, cupping Hunter's chin in her hands.

"Sure," he replied.

"And don't forget. I'll help," said Kerry. "I'll tell Mary Anne anything she needs to know. About Hunter or his allergies or — "

"Dear," Logan's father interrupted, tapping Mrs. Bruno on the shoulder, "we're going to be late. We'd better go."

"Oh, right," she agreed, and Kerry looked frustrated.

The Brunos left then, Mrs. Bruno calling instructions over her shoulder as they grabbed their tennis rackets and dashed out the back door.

I looked at Kerry and Hunter. I was just about to suggest that the three of us go to Hunter's room, when Hunter said, "Let's play hide-ad-seek. That's a good gabe. We cad all play."

"Huntie, no!" exclaimed Kerry. "You can't go running and hiding all over the house. Think of it. The basement."

"Oh, the basebet," said Hunter. "Ah-choo!"

"And hiding behind curtains."

"Curtids. Ah-*choo!*"

"And lying on rugs and in back of couches."

"Rugs. Couches. Ah-ah-ah-ah-CHOO!"

"You'd be better off outside," said Kerry.

"Oh, doe. Dot outside. There's grass ad leaves ad — ad pollid."

"Pollid?" I repeated.

"He's trying to say 'pollen,' " Kerry whispered.

"Hunter," I said. "Kerry. Let's go upstairs. We can play in Hunter's room. Hunter, you'll be more comfortable."

Even though he had wanted to play hide-and-seek, Hunter looked relieved at the suggestion. Poor thing. It must be terrible to be so uncomfortable for so long. The thought reminded me of Tigger. Where was he? Was

44

he uncomfortable? Was he stuck somewhere? Or was he off having the time of his life?

"Bary Adde?" We had reached the upstairs hallway, and Hunter was pulling at my shirt. "Look at our doors," he was saying. "At Logad's ad bide."

I looked. They were closed.

"We have to keep theb closed," said Hunter thickly, because by roob is dust-free, and Logad's is — "

"A pigsty," supplied Kerry. Then she added hastily, "I think I'll close mine, too. And keep it closed. My — my room doesn't get cleaned too often."

She opened the door to Hunter's room. "You guys go on in," she said. "I'll be right there. I just have to do something in my room and then close the door."

Kerry left. She certainly was being helpful. If all the kids I sit for were like her, my job would be a cinch.

Hunter and I went inside, closed his door — and I drew in my breath. I'd been in his room before, but I'd forgotten just how bare it is. Bare floor, bare walls, no curtains or bedspread or knickknacks. Hardly even any toys. Just a few in his closet. I'd go crazy in a room like his.

Hunter caught me looking around and said

brightly, "I have bore toys, but we keep theb dowdstairs."

"Oh, Hunter, I'm sure you have toys," I said, a bit too cheerfully.

Hunter plopped down on his bed. "Ah-choo!"

"Bless you," I said.

"Thack you. Do you watt to doe what I'b allergic to?"

"Sure."

"Okay, here goes. Dust, bold, pollid, cats, dogs, horsies — well, iddy kide of fur or hair, except people hair. I'b dot allergic to byself."

I smiled.

Kerry returned then. "What shall we do now?" she asked. "Is there anything I can help with?"

You could tell me why you're being so helpful, I thought. This was a new Kerry. The old Kerry was perfectly nice, but this Kerry was . . . unnatural.

"Let's just choose something to do," I said.

"Chutes and Ladders?" suggested Hunter. "Cootie?"

"How about Office?" said Kerry. "This could be your office, Huntie. No, wait. Vet. You're the vet and Mary Anne and I bring our sick pets to you."

Oh, why did Kerry have to suggest *that*, of all things?

But Hunter said, "You bead I get to be the vet? Oh — ah-choo! — goody. This is a good gabe."

"Mary Anne, you're first," said Kerry. "I'll be the assistant. Is that okay with you, Doctor Hunter?"

Hunter nodded.

So I pretended to carry a cocker spaniel into Hunter's office. "This is Duffy," I said, giving Hunter a name he could pronounce. "I think he hurt his paw. He's been limping."

Hunter held up an imaginary paw. "Huh," he said. "Just as I thought. Duffy broke his toes."

"I wonder how that happened?" I couldn't help saying.

Hunter paused. "He — he bust have acci-dettally walked idto the side of the bathtub. That's how Daddy broke his toes."

Kerry and Hunter looked at each other. They began to laugh. Even I laughed, worried as I was about Tigger.

"I'll go fix us a snack," Kerry volunteered.

"Well . . . all right," I replied. Kerry could be trusted in the kitchen.

She dashed down the stairs. Suddenly I ran

after her. "Hey, Kerry!" I called. "Does Hunter have any food allergies?"

"Just wheat. And milk. And strawberries. And seafood." (Sheesh.) "But don't worry. I know what he can eat."

A few minutes later, Kerry walked slowly into Hunter's room carrying a tray of snacks. We sat on the bare floor and ate. I tried to be extra neat. If Hunter was allergic to wheat and dust, would that make him allergic to cracker crumbs? I tried hard not to leave any around.

When we finished our snack, Kerry helpfully took the tray downstairs and tidied up the kitchen. She returned, and we continued the vet game and then played both Chutes and Ladders and Cootie. We had fun, even though Kerry kept interrupting the game to go do things in her room, but all I could think of was Tigger. Was he home yet? Was he eating from his bowl or curled up in Dad's lap?

Where was he?

CHAPTER 6

As soon as Mr. and Mrs. Bruno had returned and paid me, I jumped on my bike and made a dash for my house. Logan and I don't exactly live in the same neighborhood, so the ride took awhile. I knew it was good exercise, but I was impatient. Was Tigger home or not?

I turned into our driveway, flew to the end of it, and tossed my bike down. Then I crashed through our back door, slamming it behind me.

"Dad! Dad!"

"I'm in the den, Mary Anne."

I ran to the den. "Dad, is he back?" I asked, panting.

All my father had to do was look at me and I knew what the answer was.

No.

"He's been missing for almost twenty-four hours now," I pointed out.

Dad nodded.

"It's time to do something," I said. I didn't wait to see what Dad's reaction to that would be. I just marched into the kitchen. I'm not always great in an emergency, but right now, I knew what to do.

I called Kristy Thomas. Not only is Kristy one of my two best friends, but she's full of ideas. Good ideas. Plus, she loves pets. She was the best person I could think of to talk to.

"Tigger's *missing?*" Kristy squeaked when I'd given her the bad news.

"For almost twenty-four hours."

"Then there's only one thing to do. I'm calling an emergency meeting of the Baby-sitters Club. Can you be at Claudia's in an hour?"

"Definitely."

"Great. I'll see you there then."

The members of the Baby-sitters Club gathered in Claud's room slightly less than an hour after I got off the phone with Kristy. I couldn't believe we'd all been able to make it.

We were a somber group. I think that was because most of the club members' families have at least one pet, so my friends were imagining how they'd feel if their pets were missing. I, of course, was thinking of Tigger.

And trying not to cry. I'm a champion crier. Ask anyone in the club.

Kristy got right down to business, and for once I was glad to see her acting in charge, even slightly bossy. "We have a problem," she said briskly. "It's not a baby-sitting problem, but it effects one of the members of our club. Tigger is missing, and we have to do something about it. Mary Anne, why don't you tell us what's happened so far?"

"Well," I began. My voice quavered, so I started over again. "Well, when I came to our meeting yesterday, I left Tigger outside. He didn't want to go in. He's been outside alone a few times now, so I thought it would be okay. Only . . . only . . ."

I had to stop. I couldn't go on. I looked at the faces surrounding me. Kristy was in her director's chair, but she wasn't wearing her visor, and the pencil that was usually stuck over her ear was resting on Claud's desk. Claudia and Dawn were seated solemnly on the bed, and Jessi and Mallory were on the floor. Their knees were drawn up to their chests, their hands clasped around them, and they were looking at me sympathetically. I was seated in Claud's desk chair, facing everyone.

I cleared my throat. "Only," I said again,

"when I got back from the meeting, he wasn't around. Dad and I looked for him outside, but he didn't show up. And he didn't show up last night or today. I guess — I guess that's it."

"Oh, Mary Anne," said Dawn. "I'm so sorry."

"Me, too," murmured the other girls.

"So what are we going to do?" asked Kristy. When no one said anything, she answered her own question. "We're going to find him, that's what. We're going to pretend Tigger is a missing person."

"We could put up posters!" said Mallory.

"With Tigger's picture on them!" exclaimed Claud. "I could draw Tigger."

"Yeah, and the posters could say something like 'Lost or strayed. Gray kitten. Answers to the name of Tigger,' " added Jessi.

"We should say more about what he looks like," said Kristy. "A more complete description, I think. You know, how big he is, how old he is, his markings."

"And we should put, 'Last seen on Friday afternoon,' " I spoke up.

"Then add something about if you've found him, call Mary Anne's phone number," said Mal.

Over in the director's chair, I could see Kristy

getting another of her ideas. I'm not unusually perceptive. It's just that it's hard to miss Kristy getting excited. I could hear this big intake of breath, and then — I swear — she began wriggling around like a puppy.

Claudia saw, too, and said, "Kristy? Is there anything you'd like to tell us?"

(Dawn, Jessi, and Mal tried to hide their giggles.)

And Kristy exploded with, "Yes, I've got a great idea! We could offer a reward. Then we could add, 'Ten-dollar reward for the safe return of Tigger' to the poster. Or something like that."

Well, we had to admit — it *was* a great idea.

"Except for one thing," said Dawn, our treasurer. "Where are we going to get the money?"

"I've got four dollars," said Jessi.

"I've got three-fifty," said Claudia.

"Five-fifty," said Mal.

"Only two," said Dawn. "I just bought earrings. Sorry, Mary Anne."

I shook my head, smiling. Who cared? I couldn't believe what my friends were doing.

"I've got five sixty-four," said Kristy. "I know exactly."

"And I," I said softly, "have four seventy-five. I would spend my last penny to find

Tigger. I wish I had four *hundred* seventy-five."

Dawn was busy with a pencil and a pad of paper.

"Let's see here," she said. "Um, all together we've got . . . twenty-five dollars and thirty-nine cents!"

We gasped.

"Hold on, you guys," Dawn went on. "Let me check something." She reached for the club's treasury envelope and rooted around inside. At last she emerged with a fistful of bills and change.

"What are you doing?" asked Kristy.

"I just took four sixty-one from the treasury," Dawn replied. "If we add it to the money we're donating, our reward will be an even thirty bucks. Won't that look nice on the poster?"

Five heads nodded. And I began to cry.

"Mary Anne? What's wrong?" asked Dawn. "Don't worry. There's still plenty of money in the treasury. I just took out enough to make thirty."

"Oh, it's not that," I said, sniffling. (Claudia handed me a tissue.) "It's all of you. Donating the money you worked so hard for. I know you're saving for things. And now, you're giving up your money for Tigger."

"And," added Dawn, "for you."

Well, that started a fresh flood of tears. I was crying for me, for Tigger, but mostly because my friends were being so wonderful.

I cried until Dawn slid off of Claud's bed, crossed the room, and put her arms around me. Slowly, my tears subsided.

Just as I was getting under control again, I heard Mal say, " 'What shall we do about poor little Tigger?' "

"Huh?" said Kristy.

"It's from *The House at Pooh Corner*," she replied. "Our family's been reading it aloud. That line is the beginning of one of Pooh's hums. You know, his poemy-songs. The rest of it is about getting Tigger the tiger to eat. But that first line makes me think of Mary Anne's Tigger."

"Yeah," I said, nodding slowly. "What shall we do about poor little Tigger?"

I almost started to cry again, but Kristy said, "Come on, we have work to do. If we can get a sample poster finished, my mom could go to her office tonight and run off copies. Then we — "

"She'll go to the office on a Saturday night?" interrupted Claud.

"Maybe," replied Kristy. "For something this important. How many copies do you think I should ask her to make?"

We decided on a number. Then we got to work on the poster. When we were finished, this is what the top part looked like:

Lost or Strayed

Short-haired male kitten;
gray with tiger stripes.
Fifteen inches long, including tail.
Answers to the name of Tigger.
Last seen Friday afternoon.
If found, call KL 5-9102.

Underneath this information, Claud drew a picture of Tigger that really looked like him. She kept sending me home for photos of him so that she could work from them, but I didn't mind. I'd do anything that would help find him.

And at the bottom of the poster in huge letters we wrote:

*** $30 Reward for the safe return of Tigger ***

We laid the poster on the bed, and the six of us leaned over to look at it.

Mimi came in at that moment. "What is

picture?" she asked. (Mimi had a stroke last summer and it affected her speech.)

"It's Tigger," Claudia told her grandmother. "He's missing, and we're going to help find him."

Mimi looked puzzled. "Eggplants," was all she said. Then she left.

A moment of silence followed.

"I think the poster looks perfect," I said.

"I just hope it works," added Dawn.

"It will. It *has* to," Jessi said vehemently.

"Where will we put the posters?" asked Claud. I could tell she was trying not to think about Mimi. I hoped she knew the rest of us didn't mind the funny little things that happened.

"Oh, we'll put them on phone poles, in people's mailboxes. We'll go all over our neighborhood. I mean, your neighborhood," replied Kristy. "Well, I better call Charlie for a ride. Let's meet back here at noon tomorrow."

We agreed to the plan and I ran home, hoping to find Tigger.

No Tigger.

I called Logan instead and gave him the news.

"Gee, that's too bad," he said vaguely.

That was it? Tigger was missing and Logan said, "Too bad"? Where was his brain?

"Logan, he's been missing for twenty-four hours."

"I'm really sorry. . . . Oh! Darn. Now I see."

"See what?"

"What went wrong in practice today. I'm watching tapes of our games."

I couldn't believe it. But I just calmly said good-bye and hung up.

CHAPTER 7

Okay, so baby-sitting
for my brother and sister
is an easy job. I can't
help it if Becca and
Squirt are as good as
gold. Usually. Anyway,
they're sweet and easygoing
when they're at home. When
they're not at home, watch
out! You never know what
could happen. But on that
Saturday night, the three of
us were at home together
and everything was fine.
Mama and Daddy had gone
to a party for Daddy's company
and were going to be home
late. I was asleep on the

couch when they got back. That often happens.

But that was the end of my job. The beginning was suppertime. Suppertime with Becca is easy as pie. Suppertime with Squirt is one big mess....

I could tell, just from reading this notebook entry, how close Jessi and Becca and Squirt are. That is so nice. Boy, do I wish for a brother and sister. Or for just one of them.

Or for Tigger.

Anyway, as soon as Mr. and Mrs. Ramsey left, Becca said to her big sister, "Jessi, I'm hungry."

"I know," replied Jessi. "Me, too. But I want to give Squirt his supper first. I think that'll be easier. Then you and I can eat together when he's finished."

"Okay," said Becca reluctantly. She didn't want to wait — but she did want to eat dinner with Jessi.

Jessi fixed Squirt a cheese sandwich and some grapes. She cut the sandwich into small pieces, since Squirt is learning to feed himself. Then she put the food in Squirt's airplane dish, set the dish and a bottle of milk on the kitchen table, sat Squirt in his high chair, and placed his dinner in front of him.

Squirt smiled.

He picked up a piece of sandwich. He opened it. He put the cheese in his mouth and let the bread fall to the floor. Then he mashed a grape in his hands. And laughed.

"Der-bliss!" he cried.

He took another grape, tried to bite it in half, and sent it sailing across the room. More laughter.

Half an hour later, Squirt's bottle was empty. So was his airplane tray. But cheese was squished in his hair, his hands were covered with mashed grapes, and the kitchen was littered with bread, cheese, and grapes.

"You know what?" said Jessi to her sister. "I don't think he ate anything. He drank his milk. Well, he did eat that one piece of cheese, but everything else is somewhere in the kitchen."

Becca giggled. "The best part was when he shot that grape at me. Right out of his mouth. And right at my nose. I know he did it on purpose."

Becca helped Jessi clean the kitchen. Then Jessi cleaned up Squirt. And then she and her sister sat down to their own supper while Squirt watched them from his playpen.

"*We* get toasted cheese sandwiches," said Becca happily.

"Yes," replied Jessi, "because we're older and know how to eat. But if you spit anything across the table at me — I'll make you sit in the high chair."

Becca giggled.

They began to eat.

"What shall we do about poor little Tigger?" murmured Jessi a few moments later.

"What do you mean?" asked Becca.

Jessi told her about Pooh's hum, and about the missing Tigger.

"Gosh, that's awful," said Becca. "You know who's going to be really upset? I mean, besides Mary Anne?"

"Who?"

"Charlotte. She loves Tigger. She wishes Tigger were hers."

"I can understand that. Tigger's pretty cute. And Charlotte doesn't have a pet."

"I'm sure glad Misty lives in his cage," said Becca. "*He* can't run away."

Misty is the Ramseys' hamster. He's their first pet ever. Jessi and Becca think he's so adorable they could practically eat him up. He *is* cute. Because he's young, he's very small. Everything about him is tiny and adorable. (Kind of like Tigger). He's got itty-bitty feet with claws on them you can barely see. And by his nose, which is pink, are pale, pale whiskers. They're almost transparent. Misty is also pretty. His fur is patches of golden brown and white, and his eyes are shiny and black.

Guess how Jessi got Misty. She didn't go to a pet store and buy him. He came from some of her neighbors, the Mancusis. They were going away on vacation and needed a pet-sitter. So they called the Baby-sitters Club! Ordinarily, Kristy doesn't like for us club members to pet-sit, but Jessi had a free week, so she took the job — and found herself caring for cats, dogs, hamsters, rabbits, a disgusting snake that got loose one afternoon, some fish, and I don't remember what else. Anyway, while she was on the job, she discovered that one of the hamsters was going to have babies. Misty is one of those babies, of course, and the Mancusis were delighted to let Jessi have him. (By the way, Mal's family also took a hamster baby.)

"I'm glad Misty lives in a cage, too," said Jessi. "Being cooped up might seem cruel, but at least it's safe."

"Hey!" cried Becca. "I just got an idea. Maybe the Mancusis have a kitten they could give to Mary Anne. I mean, if Tigger doesn't come back."

"Maybe . . ." Jessi replied slowly. "Two of their cats are going to have kittens."

"One of the kittens might look like Tigger!" exclaimed Becca.

"Maybe," Jessi said again. Then, "I'm just wondering about one thing. Would Mary Anne want another kitten? I mean, let's say something happened to Misty — "

"What would happen to Misty?" cried Becca.

"Nothing. I'm just saying *if* something happened — "

"If what happened?"

Becca had put her sandwich down on her plate. She looked worriedly at her sister.

Jessi sighed. "Nothing. But think of it this way: If you didn't have Misty, would you want a different hamster? Sort of as a replacement?"

"No way!"

"Okay. That's what I'm thinking about with Mary Anne and Tigger. I'm not sure she'd want a replacement kitten. Not right away."

"But it's nice to know the Mancusis are here," said Becca.

"Yeah," agreed Jessi. "It's nice to know they're here."

"Ah-choo! Ah-choo!" called Squirt from his playpen. He was standing up, his arms hanging over the sides, looking at his big sisters.

Jessi and Becca began to giggle. Squirt's

newest trick is pretending to sneeze. Only his sneezes don't sound real. He just yells, "Ah-choo!" which sometimes comes out "Ah-shoo!" or even "Ah-too!"

"Hey, Squirt," said Becca, "if you eat all your vegetables, will you get" (she lowered her voice dramatically) "big . . . and . . . strong?"

Squirt's face broke into a dimply smile. Then he squeezed his hands into fists, and posed his arms like a strongman.

Jessi and Becca were now giggling so hard they could barely eat. But they calmed down. As they finished their dinners, Becca said, "Jessi, can I help Squirt walk later?"

"Sure," answered Jessi, wondering why her sister had even asked. Squirt was a new and unsteady walker, but Becca had helped him toddle around plenty of times.

"Oh, goody," replied Becca. She was quick to help Jessi with the dishes. Then she ran to Squirt's playpen and lifted him out.

Squirt squealed with happiness.

"Jessi, Jessi, come watch Squirt!" called Becca.

Jessi was sponging off the table. "Becca, I've *seen* him walk."

"Well, you haven't seen this. *Please* come here."

"Okay." Jessi abandoned the sponge and crossed the room to her brother and sister.

Becca had set Squirt on the carpeted floor of the rec room and he stood there unsteadily. She backed away. "Okay, Squirtles," she said. "Come here!" She held out her hands. "Come here!"

Squirt lurched toward Becca. As he walked, he cheered himself on. "Yea! Yea! Yea!"

So *that* was what Becca had wanted Jessi to see. Jessi began to laugh. "Who taught him that?"

"He did. I kept cheering for him when he was walking. Now he cheers for himself."

"Group hug!" announced Jessi. She and Becca and Squirt moved together for a three-person hug.

After that, it was Squirt's bedtime. Jessi read him some nursery rhymes before he went to sleep. Squirt is too little to understand them, but Jessi thinks reading is important at any age. Then she let Becca read to her from *Baby Island*, and finally, when Becca was asleep, too, Jessi brought her copy of *Sounder* downstairs and curled up with it on the living room couch. *Sounder* is about a dog, but Jessi found herself thinking of Tigger the cat, wondering the same things I was wondering. What had happened to him? Was he safe? Was he hurt? If he was hurt somewhere, would we find him? And . . . *where was he?*

CHAPTER 8

"Mary Anne, Mary Anne! My mom did it!"

"Did what?" It was Sunday morning and I hadn't been awake very long. My brain was barely working. All I knew was that Kristy was on the other end of the line and she was very excited.

"She copied the posters!" said Kristy. "I've got the whole stack right here in my lap. So I'm on my way over. We can paper the neighborhood."

I wanted to find Tigger more than anyone else did. But it was only eight-thirty in the morning. I wasn't dressed. And I had a pretty good idea that Claudia and Dawn weren't even awake. All I said, though, was "Paper the neighborhood? What does that mean?"

"You know, put up the posters. Distribute them. Cover the neighborhood with them."

"Oh. . . . Wow, Kristy, it was awfully nice of your mom to go to her office last night. She had to go all the way into Stamford, just for the posters."

"Well, Tigger is important."

"Thank you," I said, "and listen, I can't wait to start, um, papering the neighborhood. But don't you think it's a little early in the day? I'm still in my nightgown. And . . . and . . . okay, I'm walking across Dad's room, now I'm looking out the window . . . Yup, Claud's shades are down. I'm sure she's still asleep. I bet Dawn is asleep, too. And I'd kind of like to call Logan. Maybe he'll come help us. Can we meet at noon?"

"Noon?" repeated Kristy. She sounded slightly disappointed. "Well, okay. And how's this? I'll phone Jessi, Mal, and Claud, if you'll phone Dawn and Logan. Tell them to meet in your yard at twelve o'clock."

"Deal."

At noon that day, I was standing in my yard. Well, I wasn't just standing in it, I was calling for Tigger. It was impossible for me to be almost anywhere without calling or looking for him.

"Ti-i-i-igger! Here, Tiggy, Tiggy!"

I called. I whistled. I shook his toys. I set out cat food. No Tigger.

So I was relieved when the Thomases' old

station wagon pulled up in front of our house. Kristy hopped out and Charlie waved to me.

I waved back.

In Kristy's hands was a stack of papers.

"Oh, let me see," I cried, running to her. Kristy handed me the paper on the top of the stack. "Great. This is great, Kristy. How can I thank you?"

"You're my best friend. We don't have to thank each other for things. But it *would* be nice if the posters brought Tigger back."

"I'll say."

As we stood looking at the LOST OR STRAYED heading, Claudia showed up. Then Dawn and Mallory. And soon, everyone was gathered in my yard.

Kristy, holding the posters, was in her element. She was in charge.

"Now," she began, "the idea is to paper the neighborhood. By tonight, there shouldn't be a single person in this area who doesn't know that Tigger is missing. I've got boxes of thumbtacks, and I want you to make sure you put a poster on every phone pole. Maybe two posters — front and back. Then stuff mailboxes. There are plenty of streets around here."

The seven of us set out. Logan and I went as a team.

"Mary Anne?" said Logan, as we pushed

thumbtacks into opposite sides of a phone pole. "I'm really sorry about Tigger."

Well, that was a relief. "You are?" I asked.

"Sure."

"I think," I said slowly, "that this is the worst thing that's ever happened to me."

Logan smiled. "Oh, come on. Don't be so dramatic, Mary Anne. A lost kitten is sad, but aren't you overreacting a little?"

I had nothing to say to that.

Across the street, Mallory stuck a poster in a mailbox, closed the box, ran to the next one, and expertly tossed another poster in.

"Hey!" I called. "Are you training for the Poster Olympics?"

Mal grinned. "I just figure that the faster we get the posters out, the faster we'll find Tigger." She ran ahead.

Logan and I were putting posters in mailboxes when my dad drove by. He waved as he slowed to a stop.

"These are the posters, Dad!" I said, handing him one.

My father nodded. "Very profes — Thirty dollars reward! That's impressive. Where did the money come from?"

"A little came from the club treasury, but most of it's our own. We chipped in."

70

"It certainly ought to get people looking."

"You think so? Great!"

"I'm on my way to the grocery store," said Dad. "We ran out of a few things. How would you like me to take along some of the posters? I could put one on the bulletin board in the grocery store, and one on the board by the newsstand. Maybe some other stores will be open. They might let me tape a poster in their windows."

I gaped. This was *my* father? He hates doing things like that — asking for favors and stuff. "That would be terrific, Dad," I said, "but are you sure you want to?"

"For Tigger, anything."

"Okay." I handed Dad a bunch of posters and thanked him six times. He drove off.

Logan and I continued. When we reached an intersection, he turned left and I turned right. I was on my own. I walked quickly, so quickly that after a couple of blocks, my legs ached. But it was worth it for Tigger.

Oh, Tiggy, where are you? I thought. That question had been worrying me since Friday. *Where are you?* But there was another question that was even worse. It had been worrying me since Friday, too. It was so bad, I could hardly bear to think of it. The question was, Tigger, are you alive? What if Tigger had wandered away? What if he'd been hit by a car? The driver wouldn't know whom Tigger belonged to. So he'd take my kitten to a vet and explain what had happened, and the vet would say, "I'm sorry, there's nothing we can do," and then they'd get rid of Tigger. They'd have to. He doesn't wear a collar with tags.

Dead, I said to myself as I walked along. Dead, dead, dead.

I stuck a poster in a mailbox.

Dead, dead, dead.

I came to a phone pole. Time for the thumbtacks. I pulled the box from my pocket and stuck a poster to the street side of the pole. I was putting one on the opposite side when a voice said, "Who's Tigger?"

I jumped a mile. When I turned around, I found a boy who looked as if he were about ten years old. He was peering around me at the poster.

"Tigger's my kitten," I told him, trying to calm down.

The boy nodded seriously.

"Have you seen him?" I asked.

"Maybe. I guess you want him back pretty badly, don't you?"

"Oh, *yes*," I said.

"Is there really a reward?"

"Yup."

"Well then, okay. Yester- um, no, let's see. The day before yesterday I saw a — a gray kitten with tiger stripes."

"That's just like Tigger!" I cried.

"And he had short hair — I'm sure it was a he, not a she — and he was, oh, about fifteen inches long — I mean, including his tail. And, um, he answered to the name of Tigger."

I looked suspiciously at the poster I'd just put up. "How did you know to call him Tigger?" I asked the boy.

"Because his name was on his collar?" he suggested.

I shook my head. "Sorry. He doesn't wear a collar."

The boy didn't look a bit uncomfortable about having told a whopping lie. "What's the reward for?" he wanted to know. "For information leading to finding this cat or something?"

"No," I replied crossly. "For *finding* him. For putting him in my hands."

I stuffed the thumbtacks back in my pocket. Then I just walked off. *Sheesh*. What was wrong with people? Was money the only thing they could think of?

I walked and walked. I papered our neighborhood until I ran out of posters. Then I went home. I found Mal, Jessi, and Dawn sitting on my front lawn.

"We're done!" Jessi announced.

"I was done first," Mal added proudly.

I sat down with them, but as soon as I'd done so, Dawn jumped up.

"We shouldn't be just sitting here," she said. "We should be looking for Tigger."

"But I've looked and looked."

"Then we should look some more. He's just a baby. He's so little. Maybe he got stuck somewhere."

The search for Tigger started out with just the four of us. We grew to seven as Logan, Claudia, and Kristy returned. Then Charlotte Johanssen came by and she joined us. Jamie, Myriah, and Gabbie were about to start a game of Superman Tag (whatever that is), and Nicky Pike was out for a bike ride with his friend Matt Braddock, but all of them stopped their fun and helped us look for Tigger. I was just telling Logan about the boy I'd met while I was putting up posters, when Jamie pulled on my sleeve.

"Mary Anne! Mary Anne!" he said urgently.

I stooped down to his level.

"What's up, Jamie?"

"Nicky Pike said if you find Tigger you get thirty dollars."

"That's true."

"If I had thirty dollars, I'd buy eleven hundred racing cars."

I sighed. Here we go again, I thought.

"But you know what?" Jamie went on. "I'd rather just have Tigger back."

I gave Jamie a *huge* hug.

CHAPTER 9

We did not find Tigger that afternoon. Somehow, I wasn't surprised.

But I was surprised the next afternoon when Jamie Newton said to me, "Let's look for Tigger some more."

It was Monday. I was baby-sitting for Jamie and Lucy, and the weather was gorgeous. Being outdoors would feel wonderful. But it seemed to me as if we'd already looked everywhere for Tigger. Every possible place. At least around here, and I couldn't very well take the Newton kids to some other neighborhood in order to go kitten-hunting.

"Don't you want to find Tigger?" asked Jamie.

"Of course I do!" I said.

"Then let's look some more. We might have missed a place. Or maybe . . . *maybe*" (Jamie's eyes were widening at whatever this new thought was) "he's moved, and he's sitting right in some place we already checked! He might be, you know. We better look everywhere all over again."

I smiled at Jamie. "Is this really what you want to do today?"

"Yup. You can put Lucy in her stroller. And when we get to your house, we'll ask Myriah and Gabbie if they want to help us look, too."

"Well," I said slowly. "All right."

When Jamie had made his suggestion, he was sitting at the kitchen table drinking grape juice and eating crackers. And Lucy had just woken up from a nap. So there was a lot to do before we could go Tigger-hunting. I changed Lucy, cleaned her up, and put a new outfit on her. (The lavender overalls she'd worn in the morning were covered with milk, grape juice, and mashed banana.) Then I packed a bag to take on our walk. When you're watching a baby, you can't go anywhere without a bag. In it I put Baby Wipes, a bottle full of apple juice, a pacifier, a spare diaper, and a toy.

When Lucy was ready to go I started in on Jamie. He had a gigantic grape juice mustache, which we got rid of with some scrubbing. Then I found his jacket. "Do you have to go to the bathroom?" I asked him as I picked up Lucy and her bag.

"Nope," said Jamie.

"Okay." Lucy's stroller was in the garage. At the garage door, I stopped to put her sweater on. "Are you sure you don't have to go to the bathroom?" I asked Jamie again.

"I'm sure."

We went into the garage. I settled Lucy in the stroller and hung her bag on the back. "Last chance for the bathroom," I said to Jamie.

"I'm fine," he replied.

We set off. We were halfway down the driveway when Jamie said, "Mary Anne? I have to go to the bathroom."

I sighed. But what can you do? Back we went. Ten minutes later we were on our way again. When we reached the Perkinses' house, Jamie rang their bell.

"No woof-woof," he remarked.

"Chewbacca must be in the backyard," I told him. (Chewy is the Perkinses' big black Labrador retriever. He loves people and gets excited when the bell rings. Usually, you hear galloping feet and excited barks when you push the doorbell.)

But very small footsteps approached this time. Then the door opened a crack and Gabbie peeked out. When she saw us, her face broke into a grin. She threw the door open.

"Hi!" she cried, blonde hair bouncing.

"Hi-hi!" Jamie replied excitedly. "Do you

and Myriah want to look for Tigger again? Mary Anne's here. She'll help us."

"Okay. Let me ask Myriah."

The excitement over looking for Tigger was great, and in moments, Jamie and his pals were in my front yard.

"This is where you last saw Tigger, right, Mary Anne?" asked Myriah.

I nodded. "That's right."

"Then we'll start here."

Myriah, Jamie, Gabbie, and I began whistling and calling and looking in trees and under bushes. But when I pushed Lucy's stroller into the backyard and found myself looking in our toolshed, a place I was sure I had checked at least twelve times already, I began to feel discouraged — and sort of disgusted.

"Lucy-Goose," I said, and Lucy strained her neck back to see me. She answers to that name as well as to Lucy and Lucy Jane, which is her full name. "Lucy Goose, let's go get the mail. I'm tired of this." And I'm afraid, I thought. I'm afraid that someone will find Tigger — dead.

Getting the mail is the highlight of any day for me, and I felt I needed the highlight just then. So I wheeled Lucy around to the front of my house and down the driveway. I opened the box. I looked inside. Stuffed! I absolutely

adore a stuffed mailbox. I listened to the cries
and shouts of Jamie, Myriah, and Gabbie while
I struggled to pull everything out of the box.
Then I pushed Lucy up to our front stoop,
where I sat down and dropped the mail into
my lap. There was so much it overflowed and
fell on the ground. Lucy laughed as I tried to
pick it up.

At last it was stacked neatly next to me. I
sorted it into piles: bills for Dad, letters for
Dad, magazines, catalogues, stuff we could
probably throw out, letter for me. . . . Wait a
sec. A letter for me?! I hardly ever get letters.

I picked up the envelope. It must be from
Stacey, I thought. But, no, the address wasn't
in her handwriting. Ooh, very exciting. A
mystery letter!

"Now this," I told Lucy, "is why I like
getting the mail. You never know what you
might find. I can't wait to see who this letter's
from."

Lucy blew me a raspberry, then smiled
angelically.

I opened the envelope.

What I found inside gave me goose bumps.

"On, no," I cried softly.

Written in big, messy writing was a short
message:

> If you want to see your cat
> alive again, leave $100 in an
> envelope on the big rock
> in Brenner Field at 4:00
> tomorrow afternoon.

A picture of Tigger was taped to the bottom of the page. It had been cut from one of the posters we'd made.

I swallowed, feeling sick. So Tigger had been *kidnapped?* But why? Because someone needed a hundred dollars?

"This is curious," I said to Lucy. What I meant was that it was chilling, horrible, disgusting, and the meanest thing in the world — only I couldn't say that in front of a little baby.

But what was I *do*ing? Tigger had been kidnapped, and I was sitting on my front steps, talking to Lucy. I jumped up, dumped the mail in our front hall, then found Jamie and the Perkins girls.

"Listen, I'm sorry," I said to Jamie, "but it's time to go home."

"Good," he replied. "We're bored. And I have to go to the bathroom."

"Again?" I said. "Then let's go." We walked

Gabbie and Myriah to their house, then returned to the Newtons'.

I felt shaky all over by that time. I had to do something, but what? What do you do when someone is asking for a whole lot of money in order to give back something you love — and you haven't got the money? My friends and I had just barely been able to scrape together thirty dollars. There was a little more money in the treasury, but nothing close to seventy dollars. Maybe I could use the thirty dollars reward money and borrow seventy dollars from Dad. He must have seventy dollars in the bank. I could pay him back later from money I earned baby-sitting.

Okay. There was the solution. I felt a little calmer.

I was standing in the kitchen next to the telephone. From there, I could see into the Newtons' family room, where Jamie was watching *Sesame Street* and Lucy was sitting in her playpen. I hated to leave them there, but I was going to have to, for a few minutes anyway.

I picked up the phone. I dialed Dad's office. First I got cut off. Then I got a busy signal — three calls in a row. When I finally reached my father's secretary, she said he was on an important call, dear, and would I please hold?

I told her that no, I wouldn't, thank you. As I hung up, I thought, *my* call was important, too.

But maybe this was better. Maybe telling Dad about Tigger's ransom note wasn't a good idea. Dad's a lawyer. He would probably freak out, and he certainly wouldn't allow me to go to Brenner Field the next day.

I made another call. This one was to Logan. Kerry answered the phone, sounding quite cheerful, and handed me over to her big brother, who was actually home, which I hadn't really expected. He plays so much ball these days that he's usually on the field at school.

"Hi," I said glumly.

"Hi," he replied, just as glumly.

"You'll never guess what happened. Tigger has been kidnapped."

"What?" (That wasn't the "What?" I'd been hoping for. I'd been hoping for a *"WHAT??!"*)

"That's right," I went on. "They left a ransom note."

I read it to Logan. Then, tearfully, I added, "Oh, Logan, what are we going to do?"

"We?"

"Well, you and I and the rest of the Baby-sitters Club."

There was a pause. "I'll have to think," replied Logan.

"We have a club meeting today," I told him hopefully.

Another pause. "All right. I'll be there. I guess it would make sense to discuss the problem together."

"Thanks, Logan," I said. "I'll call Kristy and tell her what's going on. She should have been the one to ask you to the meeting, but I think she'll understand about this. It's an emergency." (Kristy loves emergencies.)

Logan and I got off the phone then so I could call Kristy. She was completely understanding. Certainly more so than Logan. I couldn't help thinking that he didn't seem concerned. And that hurt. But when I told Kristy about the ransom note, I got the *"WHAT??!"* I'd been waiting for.

"See you at five-thirty," said Kristy, as we were getting off the phone. "And don't worry. We're going to get Tigger back. The Baby-sitters Club can do anything."

CHAPTER 10

Mrs. Newton came home at 5:15 that afternoon, so I made it to Claudia's house just a few minutes before the beginning of our club meeting. I brought the ransom note with me, envelope and all. (Once, near Halloween, I had received a mysterious chain letter. The other girls were really upset with me for throwing away the envelope it had arrived in, so I was careful to keep the envelope from the ransom note.)

When we had all gathered, even Logan, we sat in Claud's room sort of stiffly. This always happens when Logan comes to a meeting. It's because he's a boy. Even though we know him and like him (especially me!), he just makes a meeting different. We worry about things such as what if Logan sits on something lumpy and it turns out to be some of Claudia's underwear? Or what is someone says "bra" or starts to tell a story about a girl we know who might be going out with a friend of Logan's? Not that Kristy lets much of that go on during meetings, but it does happen from time to time.

Anyway, Kristy got the opening business over with fast. Then she said, "Today is going to be a combination regular club meeting and an emergency meeting. We'll take job calls, but in between, we'll try to figure out how to handle the ransom note."

For some reason, that made me burst into tears. "Oh, that is so wonderful of you guys," I said. "You're the best friends in the world." I paused. "But where are we going to get seventy dollars?"

Logan was sitting right next to me on the bed, which squished us next to Dawn and Claudia, but he didn't do anything when I started to cry. So Claudia, on the other side of me, patted my arm and then gave me a hug. I had the feeling she wanted to give Logan a dirty look while she was at it.

"Let's not worry about the money just yet," said Kristy as I was drying my eyes. "For starters, we should take a look at the ransom note."

"Yeah," said the others.

But the phone rang then and we had to stop

to schedule a job. When we were finished, I pulled the note out of my pocket.

"I saved the envelope," I said pointedly.

My friends smiled. They knew what I was talking about.

I took the note out and laid it and the envelope side by side on the bed. Everyone crowded in for a look.

"It's those first words that scare me," I said. "They're so threatening. 'If you want to see your cat alive again . . .' It sounds like, well, if anything goes wrong, then Tigger will be . . . will be . . . Oh, I can't say it. Or maybe he already is . . . dead."

My tears started to fall again and I glanced hopefully at Logan, but he was staring off into space.

"Well," said Jessi, "the handwriting on the envelope and on the note are the same."

"But is this the real thing or some kind of trick?" asked Claudia, our mystery expert. "Any time there's a missing person, it seems as if about a million ransom notes suddenly turn up."

"Yeah," agreed Mallory.

"It seems to *me*," Dawn spoke up, "that if the kidnapper wanted us to know he was the real one, he would have given us a better clue.

For instance, an actual photo of Tigger — you know, a Polaroid — to show he's alive now. Not just his picture cut from the poster we made. Anyone could do that."

"Also," said Mallory, "the posters have been up for two days. If someone really was going to take advantage of them, he — or she — could have written the note Saturday afternoon and delivered it to Mary Anne yesterday morning. Why wait?"

"Was that note mailed or just stuck in your box?" Logan asked me suddenly.

"Just stuck in the box," I replied. I handed him the envelope. "See? No stamp."

He nodded.

The phone rang again. Dawn saw that I was still a wreck, so she took the club record book out of my lap and scheduled what might well be the one and only job she'd ever schedule.

While the others were busy with the call, Logan looked over at me and whispered, "Mary Anne, would you calm down? You are being so . . . sensitive. You're acting like such a *girl*."

For a moment, I just glared at him. "There's nothing wrong with being sensitive," I told him, "and besides, I *am* a girl."

Claudia hung up the phone then, so Logan and I fell silent.

"The question is," said Kristy, "what are we going to do? I don't think we should worry about whether the note is a hoax. I think we should just follow up on it. It's our only lead."

"Right!" agreed Logan. "We should go to Brenner Field and get this jerk who took Tigger. We'll beat him at his own game."

"But how?" asked Dawn.

We stopped talking to think and to take two calls that came in.

Then, in a very small voice, and even though I had just been thinking the opposite an hour earlier, I said, "Maybe I should tell my dad about — "

"No!" exclaimed Logan. "We're not involving any adults. No parents, no police."

"Why not?" I asked.

"Because they'll just get in the way. A kid wrote that note. Don't you think so? Look at that big, babyish handwriting. And an adult would want more than a hundred dollars. Why would a grown-up go to all the trouble of stealing a kitten for three days, just to get a hundred dollars? It's not worth it."

"That's true," the rest of us agreed.

"So?" said Kristy.

"Well," Logan went on slowly, "we don't know if that note is from an actual kidnapper, or just from someone trying to take advantage of Tigger's situation, but either way we should catch him — "

"Or her," added Dawn.

" — or her. Don't you think?"

I looked at my friends. We all nodded. This was getting sort of exciting.

"How are we going to catch the kidnapper?" wondered Jessi.

Logan frowned thoughtfully. He read the ransom note again. " 'In an envelope on the big rock in Brenner Field at four o'clock,' " he mused. "Do you know what the big rock is?" he asked the rest of us. "I don't even know where Brenner Field is."

"It's right nearby," Claudia told him. "That's probably why you don't know it. It's not in our neighborhood. It's sort of behind Jamie Newton's backyard."

"And do you know this big rock?" asked Logan.

"Oh, sure," I replied. "Everyone does. There's a boulder near one side of the field. We just call it the 'big rock.' "

Logan nodded. "Listen, you guys," he said to the six of us girls, "I'm getting an idea, but I'm going to need the help of all of you — or most of you — tomorrow."

"We'll be there," said Kristy, without even looking at the record book.

"But Kristy!" I cried. "We've probably got jobs — "

"This is too important. We'll look at the record book in a minute. Then we'll reschedule whatever needs rescheduling."

"Okay." (Why was I protesting? I was the one who wanted Tigger back so badly.)

"Well," said Logan, "this is my idea. Mary Anne goes to the rock at four, just like the note says to do. She leaves an envelope full of money — "

"What money?" I interrupted.

"Fake money. Monopoly money or something."

"Well, as long as I'm not putting real money in the envelope, why do I have to bother with fake? Why can't I just stuff an envelope with newspaper or notebook paper?"

"I don't know," said Logan irritably. "Fake money is what they always use on TV or in the movies. Maybe it looks more realistic from the outside. Don't ask me."

"So go on," said Kristy. "Mary Anne stuffs an envelope with fake money — "

"Not *too* much," I interrupted. "It's only a hundred dollars. Ten ten-dollar bills wouldn't look very fat. The envelope shouldn't be too stuffed."

"Mary Anne!" cried Claudia in exasperation.

"Sorry," I said, "but we're talking about Tigger. I want this to go right."

Kristy sighed. "Logan?" she said. "After Mary Anne fills the envelope?"

"Then way before four, like pretty soon after we get home from school, the rest of us hide in Brenner Field, in places where we can see the big rock. Is that possible?"

"To hide in the field or to find places you can see the rock from?" asked Mal.

"Both," replied Logan.

"Yes," said Mal.

"Great. Okay, so we hide. At four o'clock, Mary Anne leaves the envelope on the rock. Then, Mary Anne, you better pretend to go home, in case you're being watched. Actually, you should probably go all the way home. But then sneak back to the field. I think you'll want to see what happens next. I have a feeling the kitten-napper will turn up. And we can catch him."

It was a thrilling plan. I was so proud of Logan! We were talking and thinking of hiding places in the field when Kristy remembered the record book. I was the one who'd been so worried about it — and then I'd forgotten.

"We have to find out what we're doing tomorrow," said Kristy. "If a lot of us are baby-sitting, then we have a problem, because we can't all cancel."

As it turned out, only one of us was sitting and we got Shannon Kilbourne to go in her place. Some of the others had classes or lessons but decided not to go. We would all be at Brenner Field the next afternoon.

My heart began to beat a little faster. This was exciting! It was like something from a cop show on TV. We were going to trick the kidnapper. He had tried to get us, and now we were going to get him back. Tigger would be returned to us *and* we'd teach the kitten-napper a big fat lesson.

As we left the meeting, my excitement grew. But all of a sudden, I felt terrible. How could I feel excited? What was the matter with me? If Tigger were home, where he belonged, I'd have nothing to feel excited about. I'd just have Tigger, which is the way it should be. And I'd trade a little excitement for Tigger any day.

CHAPTER 11

Monday

Cat-napped, kitten-napped,
Tigger-napped. I've heard more
words lately describing the
disappearance of Tigger.
Not that this annoys me.
It just interests me. And
by the way, boy, does word
spread fast in a small town.
Every now and then I'm
reminded of that. The
California town I lived in is
bigger than Stoneybrook, so
it's not like the entire
neighborhood knows each
time you take a bath.

But here, well, Mary Anne
received the ransom note
this afternoon and the

Barrett kids knew about it by this evening when I baby-sat for them. They didn't know about our plan, thank goodness, but the note was enough. And were they ever spooked. . . .

Dawn didn't say so, not in her notebook entry, but she was pretty spooked herself. It was just that kind of night. The Barrett kids were upset about pet-nappers, and then the storm came.

The Barrett kids are Buddy, Suzi, and Marnie. Buddy is seven, Suzi is four, and Marnie is only a year and a half. Dawn has sat for them for quite awhile; since not too long after she moved to Stoneybrook. She likes them a lot — even though at first they were the "impossible three." Boy, did they give Dawn a hard time. But now they're much better. Buddy, who is active and lively, likes to play with Pow, their dog. Suzi likes to play pretend games. And Marnie just tries to keep up with her older brother and sister. The best thing, though, is that their mother is more organized than she used to be. (Mr. and Mrs. Barrett are divorced.) Dawn's mother is pretty disorganized herself — she's apt to put the socks away in the bread drawer. But Mrs. Barrett used to do things like forget to clean the house, or give Dawn the wrong phone number for wherever she was going while Dawn was sitting. But now she's much better. She got a job she likes a lot, and she's been trying really hard ever since then.

"Hi, Dawn!" Suzi greeted Dawn happily at the door. "Mommy said I could let you in."

Dawn entered the Barretts' house, closing the door behind her. "A storm is blowing in," she told Suzi. "It's all windy, and I can smell rain in the air."

Suzi found this hysterical. "A storm is *blowing* in?" she repeated. "You can *smell* rain in the air?"

"Yup," replied Dawn.

Marnie toddled in from the kitchen. She stared shyly at Dawn, even though Dawn has sat for her so many times.

"Where's your mom?" Dawn asked Suzi. "And where's your big brother?"

"Mommy's upstairs and Buddy's downstairs. With Pow. He's guarding him."

"Guarding him? A guard-human and his dog?" said Dawn.

"I guess so," replied Suzi, not understanding. "It's so Pow won't get bassett-napped. That's what Buddy said."

Very curious, thought Dawn. Pow is a bassett hound, that much she knew. Everything else Suzi was talking about was a mystery to her.

At that moment, Mrs. Barrett came flying downstairs. (She's usually in a rush.) "Hi, Dawn!" she said breathlessly. "Suzi, wash Marnie's face, please."

Suzi took Marnie into the kitchen and began to wash cookie crumbs off of her face.

"I'm just going to be at the office," Mrs. Barrett continued. "Special project. You've got my office number. I should be home by nine-thirty."

"Perfect," said Dawn.

"The kids should go to bed as follows: Marnie, now; Suzi, eight o'clock; Buddy, nine o'clock. No more snacks for anybody, and Buddy is allowed to watch *Dragon Warriors* on TV tonight. He asked me about it earlier, and I couldn't make up my mind. You can give him the good news. It comes on at eight."

"Okay," Dawn replied.

Mrs. Barrett left in a hurry, Marnie crying behind her. Dawn picked Marnie up and talked to her. "Your mommy's coming back. Your mommy's coming back," she kept telling her. "When you wake up tomorrow morning, guess who will be here — Mommy!"

"Dawn, will you help me guard Pow?" asked Buddy. He had placed Pow in an elaborate-looking box on which he'd drawn gears and levers. He had also wrapped string around it, stuck things to it with tape, and labeled it "Basset-Napping-Proof."

"I will as soon as I've put Marnie to bed," Dawn replied. "Is that okay? I'll be down in a little while."

"Anything's okay as long as you're not a bassett-napper," said Buddy.

So Dawn took Marnie upstairs. She gave her a bath, since Marnie loves baths.

"Moy? Moy baff?" Marnie kept asking, as Dawn played with her. (That's Marnie-talk for, "More bath?")

"A little more," replied Dawn. "Look. Here are Bert and Ernie. They're in their boat. They're sailing over to . . . Big Bird!"

Marnie laughed. Soon, though, Dawn was tired of boats and Big Bird, and Marnie's fingers were looking pruny, so Dawn lifted her out of the tub and dried her off.

"Okay, bedtime," she announced.

Marnie began to whimper. But when she'd

been tucked into her crib with her animals and her blanket, she looked quite happy.

"Good night, Marnie-O," whispered Dawn. She turned out the light and tiptoed out of Marnie's room, leaving the door open a crack. At the head of the stairs, she stopped and listened.

Nothing. Good. Marnie would fall asleep quickly.

Two flights down in the family room, Dawn found Pow still in his box. "So what is this?" she asked Buddy and Suzi.

Buddy was sitting by the box, facing in one direction, Suzi was sitting by it facing in the other. Both kids looked scared yet determined.

"We're guarding," Buddy replied. "We're not going to let Pow get dog-napped the way Tigger got kitten-napped. We heard about the letter Mary Anne found in her mailbox. We know about the kitten-napping."

Thank goodness they didn't know about Brenner Field or our plan.

"You *heard?*" exclaimed Dawn. "How? I mean, who did you hear it from?"

"Matt Braddock signed it to me." (Matt is deaf. He communicates with sign language, which most of his friends know.)

"Who did *he* get the news from?" Dawn

asked. Maybe that would be a clue to the mystery.

Buddy frowned. "Nicky Pike. Nicky said Jamie Newton told him."

"Oh," said Dawn. Darn. No clue there. "So you heard about the note," she continued.

"Yup," answered Buddy, and Suzi nodded her head vigorously.

"And you've protected Pow," Dawn went on.

"Mm-hmm. We built him this special nap-proof box. We don't want him to get napped, too," said Suzi.

"Bassett-napped," Buddy corrected her.

"Or Pow-napped," Dawn added.

"Right," agreed Buddy. "Anyway, you know what happens sometimes? Sometimes bad guys come into a neighborhood and start going around pet-napping. Mostly they take dogs and cats. They're easier because they're outdoors. And then they sell them to people who want nice pets, and the real owners of the animals never see them again."

"Unless there's a good detective," said Suzi, "and he finds the bad guys."

"Buddy, Suzi," Dawn said, "I really don't think you have to worry about this."

"Yes, we *do*," said Buddy firmly. "Sometimes there's a — a *rash* of pet-napping in a neighborhood."

"I just don't think that's going to happen here."

"It might."

"How long are you going to keep Pow indoors in this box?" asked Dawn.

Buddy frowned. "I don't know."

"How about a compromise?" Dawn suggested. "A compromise between you and Pow. Buddy, you agree that Pow doesn't have to stay in the box, and Pow will agree to go outside only when you take him — until tomorrow afternoon. After tomorrow we'll know if Tigger was really kitten-napped. If he was, there could be trouble. If he wasn't, then the note was just a joke and you won't have to worry."

"How come you'll know that tomorrow?" asked Buddy.

"We just will. Trust me," said Dawn.

"Well . . . okay." Buddy lifted Pow out of the box and Pow took off, looking as if he'd been released from prison.

"Suzi-Q," Dawn began.

"Oh, no! Please! Just ten more minutes," begged Suzi, before Dawn even said the word "bedtime."

"Sorry. It's too close to eight o'clock. We better start now. Say good night to Buddy and Pow. Then we'll go upstairs. I think we'll have time for a story."

"Okay." Reluctantly, Suzi said good night to Buddy, then found Pow and kissed his floppy ears.

Once Dawn and Suzi were in Suzi's bedroom, everything was fine. Suzi changed into her nightgown and got ready for bed. Then she chose a book to read — *Millions of Cats*. They read it twice. At last Dawn stood up.

"Okay, Suzi-Q. Time to go to sleep."

"No," said Suzi, but her eyes were already half closed.

"Sleep tight," whispered Dawn, as she turned out the light.

"Okay." Suzi's reply was so faint that Dawn could barely hear it.

Dawn dashed downstairs. The time was 8:05, and she'd just remembered something. "Buddy!" she called.

"Yeah?"

Dawn found Buddy in the playroom. He was about to open up his junior chemistry set. Perfect timing, thought Dawn. "Guess what," she said. "I forgot to tell you. Your mom said it's okay to watch *Dragon Warriors*."

"You forgot to tell me, and I forgot about the show!" Buddy laughed. "Thanks, Dawn." He abandoned his chemistry set, jumped up, turned on the TV, and was glued to it for the next half hour.

At eight-thirty, he went upstairs. Recently he has decided that he likes to get ready for bed on his own, and then put himself to bed. So he did just that. Dawn trusted him.

After he'd left, she sat in the playroom, the TV off, listening to the storm. The wind had picked up again and it howled around the house. Dawn could see lightning and hear great claps of thunder, but no rain was falling yet.

Dawn loves a good storm, but she was a little spooked — by the Tigger-napping, and by Buddy's stories of rashes of pet-nappings. Would a pet-napper, she wondered, try to break into a house to steal a dog? A bassett hound, for instance?

CRASH went the thunder!

In a flash, Dawn had picked up the phone and called me. We talked until she felt better. We talked about my dad and her mom. (No dates planned.) Then we talked about Logan.

"Poor guy," said Dawn.

"Poor guy?" I exclaimed. "He's being impossible. He's unpredictable, and he certainly hasn't been very understanding or sympathetic lately."

"He's having a hard time on the ballfield."

"He is?"

"Well . . . he did once, anyway. I happened to be watching practice, and he dropped a ball that he'd caught and had right in his mitt. The coach yelled at him, and his teammates teased him."

"So he had a bad day."

CRASH! CRASH! Lightning lit up the sky at the same time the thunder sounded.

"Dawn?" I said. "We better get off the phone. My time is up and I don't think you're supposed to use the phone during an electric storm."

Dawn sighed. "Okay."

We hung up, both of us wondering what the next afternoon would bring.

CHAPTER 12

How I made it through school on Tuesday is beyond me. All I could think about was Tigger, and our plan for the afternoon. What had we gotten ourselves into? Were we in any danger? I didn't really think so, but you never know. Maybe we were fooling around with ex-cons or something. But Logan was right — the culprit was probably a kid. And I hoped he *had* taken Tigger, so I could have him back.

At lunch that day, Kristy, Claudia, Dawn, Logan, and I sat together at a table that was as far from the crowded ones as possible. (Jessi and Mal eat during a different lunch period.) We had decided not to discuss the Tigger-napping at school, just in case the wrong person should overhear something, but Logan wanted to go over the details of our plan once more.

"Mary Anne?" he said. "You fixed the envelope?"

I nodded. "It's just a regular letter envelope. It looks like it's full of bills, though. I put in Monopoly money — fifteen tens, so it's not too stuffed."

"Good. And you know what to do today?"

"Every step of the plan."

"Great. The rest of you — you have your hiding places picked out?"

"Yup," replied Kristy. "And we'll meet up with you so I can show you your hiding place. Oh, and Mary Anne, you know where I'll be hiding, right?"

"Yes. In the tall grass behind the sycamore tree." I needed to know Kristy's hiding place so I could hide with her after I returned from pretending to go home. That way, she could give me news, if there was any, about what had happened after I'd left the envelope. I could have hidden with Logan, but he wanted to be alone in case he had to rush out and do something daring. What he didn't realize was that if he did, I'd join him in a second, followed by all the other members of the Baby-sitters Club.

We stick together.

At any rate, our plans were set.

"And now," said Kristy, "we better not talk about this anymore. We should just be our regular Baby-sitters Club table having lunch.

So in that case, anyone care for some fish eyes and glue?" she asked, holding out her dish of tapioca pudding.

I know my face turned green.

That afternoon, we all went home in whatever way we usually would, except for Kristy, who walked home with Claudia, pretending she was going over to her house for the afternoon. It was easier than going to her house and then having to come all the way back to our neighborhood.

When I reached my house, I let myself inside and pounced on the envelope I'd fixed up. I was so afraid it would be missing. (What was the big deal? I'd get another envelope and put some more Monopoly money in it.) I think I was just worried about what might happen in Brenner Field — and soon.

I looked at my watch. Three-thirty. My friends were probably already hidden.

Three forty-five. With trembling hands, I picked up the envelope. It was time to go. I had to be at the big rock by four o'clock.

I left my house, locking the door behind me, and got on my bicycle. Bicycling would be a quicker way to travel when I was pretending to come home later. Then I turned onto the street, rode past Jamie's house, stopped by a wooded area, and locked my bike to a tree. Clutching the envelope, I walked through the grove and entered Brenner Field. It was damp and muddy in places from the storm the night before. I couldn't see any of my friends. I knew they were there, but they must have been awfully well hidden.

I had to pretend I was alone, though, so I just walked through the field, heading straight for the rock. When I reached it, I looked around. Was Tigger's kidnapper somewhere nearby? Was *Tigger* nearby? I saw nothing.

I laid the envelope on the rock. I put a smaller rock on top of it to keep it from blowing away. Then I left. I walked right back through the field the way I'd come, unlocked my bike, rode home, and put the bike away.

I waited for five very long minutes. Then I dashed across the street, through Claudia's yard, through several other yards to Jamie's, and approached the field from a different direction.

Bending over to keep low, I ran to Kristy's hiding spot, a tree in the middle of the field. I sank down against the trunk and looked hopefully at Kristy.

"Good work," she whispered. "I think. I mean, everything went smoothly. Let's just hope no one saw you come back. But nothing happened while you were gone."

"Darn," I replied.

Puff, puff, Pant, pant. I worked at getting my breath back.

Kristy and I peeked around the sides of the sycamore tree. We could just barely see the big rock. We stared at it. We stared and stared and stared.

Half an hour went by.

"I guess it was a joke," I whispered at last. "Maybe someone thought we'd think the note was funny, or that we wouldn't believe it."

"Maybe Sam did it," suggested Kristy glumly.

Just as she finished speaking, I saw a flash of red across the field.

"Look!" I cried softly, pointing.

Kristy's head snapped up.

The two of us jerked to attention. We watched as a boy stepped into Brenner Field. He looked from left to right several times, as if he expected to see something . . . or someone. Then he shaded his eyes and stared toward the big rock.

"His hands are empty," I whispered to Kristy in disappointment. "He doesn't have Tigger with him."

Kristy made a sad face but didn't say anything, since we were supposedly being as quiet as possible.

The boy crept through the field, looking from left to right and behind him.

Suddenly I gasped.

Kristy looked at me around the back of the tree.

"That's the kid I met when I was putting up posters," I whispered indignantly. "He's the one who pretended he'd seen Tigger."

Kristy frowned. We returned to our watching.

The boy reached the big rock. He saw the white envelope with the stone on top, brushed the stone away, and pocketed the envelope. He didn't even look inside it. Then he began to walk off.

"Hold it!" someone shouted.

Logan leaped out of the hiding place Kristy had shown him. He ran for the boy, but the boy raced away.

In a flash, we were *all* after the kid. Logan caught up with him first and grabbed him. Then the rest of us — all six of us — surrounded him.

"Where's Tigger?" I demanded.

"Tigger?" the boy repeated.

"That's right."

"I don't know what you're talking about."

"You mean you can't remember those posters you watched me put up?"

Kristy, standing next to me, was smiling. I could imagine her saying, "Way to go, Mary Anne."

I don't usually stand up for myself.

"Oh, um," stammered the boy, "yeah, those posters. Now I remember. Tigger is a missing . . . skunk?"

"Kitten," replied Logan through clenched teeth. "And where is he?"

"Where is he?"

"Yeah. You've got your envelope," said Logan fiercely. "Now give us Tigger."

"After I see what's in the envelope."

Logan moved as quickly as a striking rattle-snake. One second the envelope was in the boy's hand, the next second it was in Logan's. "Give us Tigger and I'll give your money back," he said.

I widened my eyes. All this for Tigger? (And maybe for me?)

"Give me the money and I'll tell you where Tigger is," countered the boy.

"No way," said Kristy. "And remember, it's seven against one."

"And we can wait around all afternoon. All night, if necessary," added Jessi.

The boy scowled. "Okay, okay," he said.

Goody, I thought. Now comes the part where he tells us where Tigger is.

"I don't have your stupid cat," the boy went on. "I just said I did so I could earn some fast money."

"You little — " I began, but Dawn put her hand on my arm. I knew she meant, Don't let him know he got to you. I changed course. "What a stupid thing to do!" I exclaimed. "It didn't work, did it? You got caught, and now you look like a fool!"

"Whoa," said Kristy under her breath.

If the boy could have backed up then, I think he would have. But he turned round and saw Mallory blocking his path. No way out. He began to look scared.

"What's your name, kid?" asked Logan.

"I — I'm not telling. I mean, why do you want to know?"

"Do you know that what you did is a felony?"

I have no idea whether this is true, since Logan can make things up pretty easily, but it sure sounded good.

"It is?"

"Yes. And in the state of Connecticut, it's punishable by twenty-five to fifty years in the slammer. Even for juvenile offenders."

Now I knew Logan was just talking. He loves to use cop-show words like those.

"We could make a citizens' arrest," Logan went on. He looked around at us and we nodded as if to say, The seven of us are in agreement on *every*thing.

"Are you going to?" asked the boy. "Arrest me, I mean?"

Logan looked at us girls. Then just at me.

I shook my head. "Nope. He's not worth it." (The boy let out a breath he must have been holding for at least five minutes. That's how deep it sounded.) "So let go of him and show him the money," I said. "Let him see what he's missing."

Logan grinned. "Sure thing." He opened the envelope and pulled out the Monopoly bills.

"That's all you'd have gotten away with anyway," I told the kid.

"*That?* Fake money?" he cried.

"Well, it just goes to show," spoke up Claudia. "Crime really doesn't pay." She grinned.

Everyone laughed except the boy, who looked disgusted. We moved aside and let him escape. He ran through the field the way he had come, and disappeared. The rest of us walked back to my neighborhood.

Our adventure was over. *But where was Tigger?*

CHAPTER 13

windsday

Today I babbysat for Maria and Gabie Perkin their always fun. They whanted to play dective games, but Gabby kept saying ~~tt tt~~ Okay I'am going to spell this very carefully. She kept saying defective. Not detective, defective. Isn't that funny. You know like something is wrong. A defective detective.

Okay so the girls have made up there games and invinted Jami Newton over and their searching for Tiger. And all the time their looking, a harrible thoght is running threw my head. Mary Anne this is an awful thing to write in the notebook but I think maybe tigger is dead.....

That *was* a horrible thought, but Claudia certainly wasn't the only one to think it. I'd thought of it the very first night Tigger was gone, and it had been hanging over me like a dark cloud ever since. You can't help but wonder about the worst possibilities, yet you tell yourself all along that they could *never* happen. Anyway, Claudia's notebook entry didn't surprise or offend me.

It was Wednesday, the day after our rendezvous with the jerky kid in Brenner Field. My friends and I were trying to get back on normal schedules. I wanted to search for Tigger, but I had a feeling it would be pointless. I would just have to keep my eyes and ears open and let the posters do their work. So I was baby-sitting for Kerry and Hunter Bruno again, and Claudia was at the Perkinses'.

Myriah and Gabbie are really great kids. This is the truth. I knew it from the very first time I baby-sat for them. They adore Laura, their baby sister, they love to sing and dance, and they're very imaginative. Most kids just play house. You should see the games they invent. The afternoon that Claudia was there they played detective games.

When Claudia arrived, Mrs. Perkins reminded her where the emergency numbers were posted. Then she gave Claud a few instructions, and she and Laura left. Claudia sat down at the kitchen table, where the girls were having a snack. Her first thought as she sat down was one I always have when I'm at the Perkinses': How weird to think that this used to be Kristy's house. It doesn't look the same from the inside, and it doesn't even feel the same. I guess that's good. It would be *too* weird if it looked and felt the same as ever.

Claudia watched Myriah and Gabbie, who were dunking Oreos in glasses of milk. "What do you want to do today, you guys?" she asked.

"Gosh," replied Myriah, "there are so many things."

Claudia smiled. She wouldn't mind being five again. "Like what?" she asked.

"Like dancing or singing or making up a play."

"Sounds like fun. Which do you want to do, Gabbers?"

"Mm, let me think." Gabbie put down her glass of milk. "I would like to sing, Claudee Kishi," she replied. (Gabbie calls most people by their full names.) "I would like to sing Christmas songs."

"Christmas songs!" exclaimed Claudia. "But Christmas is months away."

"That doesn't matter," Myriah spoke up.

"I guess not," said Claudia.

Myriah and Gabbie jumped up from the table. "We know 'White Christmas,' " said Myriah. "And 'I'll Be Home for Christmas.' "

Claudia was surprised. They did? What about the simple songs like "Jingle Bells" or "Rudolph the Red-Nosed Reindeer?" But the Perkins girls know a lot of long, grown-up songs. And sure enough, they knew both of these, word for word. They performed them with hand motions and everything.

Claudia was impressed. "Hurray!" she cried, clapping her hands. "Hurray!"

The girls took bows. "Thank you, thank you," they said.

"And now," Myriah went on, as if she and Gabbie were putting on a show, "we will perform that oldy but goody, 'Blue Suede Shoes,' by Mr. Elvis Presley."

Claudia was even more impressed. Apparently, Myriah and Gabbie knew an entire rock and roll song — and she didn't. Furthermore, for years Claudia had thought the singer's name was Elbow Presley.

Gabbie and Myriah ran to their bedrooms.

They returned wearing black sunglasses and Hawaiian shirts. Then they bopped their way through the song.

"Hey!" exclaimed Myriah when they had finished, and Claudia had stopped clapping. "Gabbie, you know what we could play now?"

"What?"

"Hawaiian detectives. We're all dressed for it."

"Hawaiian defectives? What are they?"

"They're people who live in Hawaii and look for things."

"What kinds of things?"

"Missing things. Like Tigger."

"Oh."

Claudia had stood up. She was clearing the kitchen table. She put the dirty plates and cups in the dishwasher. Then she sponged off the counter and tabletop.

"Claudia?" asked Myriah suddenly. "Do real detectives look for pets?"

Claudia had no idea, but she said, "Well, I don't see why not. They look for people all the time. So I'm sure they look for animals, too."

"Oh, good."

"Come on, Claudee Kishi," Gabbie said, as Myriah led her sister outdoors.

Claudia followed the girls. As the three of them stepped onto the back porch, they were greeted by joyous woofs. There was Chewbacca, ready to play. He looked as if he wanted to say, Okay, guys. Here I am. All ready. What do we do first?

Gabbie glanced at Myriah. "Is Chewy going to be a defective, too?"

"Yes," replied Myriah. "He is. He will help us find R.C. I mean, Tigger."

Claudia smiled. R.C. is the Perkinses' cat. Claudia had a feeling the girls were going on a fake Tigger hunt. She also thought it was pretty interesting that Myriah didn't even expect to find Tigger anymore. Only a Tigger stand-in.

"Now, Gabbie," Myriah began, as she sat on the lawn with Claudia, Chewy, and her sister, "we are playing a special Hawaiian detective game called 'private eyes.' "

"Private eyes?" repeated Gabbie, puzzled.

"Don't worry about it. They're detectives. A lot of them live in Hawaii."

"Why?"

"I don't know. They just do. At least on TV. But it doesn't matter. Now, the first thing private eyes do when they've got a case is — "

"Go on the swings!" cried Gabbie. She jumped up, heading for the swing set.

"No!" exclaimed Myriah. "Don't you want to play, Gabbers?"

And Chewy looked at Gabbie with eyes that said, Oh, please, please, please, please, *please* stay and play with me!

"Okay," she replied, and sat down again.

Claudia pulled her into her lap.

"All right. There's a missing cat," Myriah began. "I mean, kitten. His name is Tigger. It's our job to find him. Are you ready for that job, Private Eye Gabbie?"

Gabbie was poking at a beetle in the grass.

"Private Eye?" Myriah asked again. "Private Eye?"

"*You're* the private eye," Claudia whispered to Gabbie.

"Oh, yeah," she said.

Sometimes we forget that Gabbie is only two and a half.

"Hmm. Maybe we need one more private eye around here," said Myriah.

Claudia didn't *really* want to play detectives, and started to say so, but before she could open her mouth, Myriah said, "Can we see if Jamie can come over?"

"Sure," replied Claudia, even though sometimes this is a good idea, and sometimes it isn't. Jamie, Myriah, and Gabbie are good friends, but every now and then they get just a tiny bit wild.

Claudia walked the girls and Chewbacca over to Jamie's house, spoke to Mrs. Newton, took Jamie by the hand, and then walked everyone back to the Perkinses'.

Myriah assembled her team in the backyard. She stood in front of Jamie and Gabbie and said once more, "We have a missing kitten. His name is Tigger. It's our job to find him. Are you ready for that job, Private Eyes?"

"Yes!" shouted Gabbie and Jamie.

"Then let's get going! Spread out, men!"

The kids searched the Perkinses' backyard. R.C. was nowhere in sight.

"Hey, Private Eye Myriah, can I look in the house?" asked Jamie.

"Sure," replied Myriah. "Good thinking!"

Claudia stood around on the porch, where she could keep an eye on both Jamie and the girls. After a few minutes, Jamie returned triumphantly to the porch, lugging R.C.

"Good work!" shouted Myriah. "Where did you find him, Private Eye?"

"In the bathroom! Napping!"

"What are you going to do with him now?" Claudia asked the private eyes.

"Give him back to Mary Anne," said Myriah.

"Oh, okay. But Mary Anne isn't home now. She's baby-sitting."

Myriah looked thoughtful. "If someone *really* found Tigger," she said slowly, "and Mary Anne wasn't home and neither was her daddy, what would happen?"

"I think the person would just wait until someone came home. Don't you? I mean, if R.C. were Tigger — if you'd found Tigger — you'd wait until someone came home, right? You'd keeping calling the Spiers' house, or ringing their doorbell. And when someone finally answered, you'd give Tigger back."

"Right," said Myriah. She and Jamie and Gabbie went back to their detective game.

Claudia sat on the porch and watched them. A funny feeling had washed over her. And that was due to the awful thought she was thinking. What if Tigger were dead? What if he were never coming back? What would I do? Claudia knew my mother had died when I was young. I don't remember her dying, but it had happened, and Claudia didn't want another death in my family. (Tigger definitely counts as family.)

Claudia worried and worried. No one she was close to had died. Mimi had gotten very sick when she'd had her stroke, but then she'd recovered, even if she was a little confused now.

But Tigger had been missing an awfully long time now, for a kitten. Five whole days.

Claudia had a bad feeling about things, overall. She wondered if it was too soon to ask me how I'd feel about getting another kitten, about getting a replacement for Tigger.

CHAPTER 14

"Ah-choo! Ah-choo!"

Guess where I was? Back at the Brunos'. Poor Hunter's allergies weren't any better than before. In fact, I thought he sounded worse.

"Thank you for coming on short notice, Mary Anne," Mrs. Bruno said to me. "Hunter was supposed to see the dentist today, too, but as you can hear, it probably wouldn't be a very good idea. He can have his teeth checked some other time."

"Yeah, but us lucky ones still get to go today," said Logan, taking Kerry's hand. "Ah. I just love the dentist."

Mrs. Bruno and I laughed, but Kerry shook her brother's hand away. "Mom," she said crossly, "do I have to go the dentist today? I'd rather stay at home."

"Honey, you've barely left the house the last few days. Besides, we have an appointment, and there's no reason to miss it."

124

"Hunter's missing it."

"Hunter has a reason. He would probably sneeze and bite the dentist."

Kerry managed a smile.

"Okay, Mary Anne, you're on your own," said Mrs. Bruno, heading for the door. "We should be back in a couple of hours."

I smiled. "Don't worry about us. Hunter and I will be fine."

"Yeah," said Hunter. "Just . . . fide. Ah-choo! Ah-CHOO!"

Mrs. Bruno shook her head. Then she and Kerry and Logan left.

"Well," I said to Hunter, "what do you feel like doing this afternoon?"

"Ridig by bike? Doe, that's probably dot — ah-choo! — a very good idea. Ub, we could go up to by roob ad play with by erector set. It's really deat. It has all this space stuff — a ludar bodule ad a bood-bobile."

It took me a moment to figure those last two things out, but finally I said, "Oh, a lunar module and a moon-mobile!"

"Right." Hunter nodded.

"Okay. Let's go."

Hunter led me upstairs to his bare room. He pulled his erector set out of the closet. We began planning our space station, but right away, Hunter's sneezing grew worse.

Maybe he's sneezing because of my perfume, I thought. I hardly ever wear perfume, but at school that day, Claudia had dabbed some of hers onto my neck and wrists. I could still smell it. "Be right back," I said. I ran into the bathroom, ripped off a sheet of paper towel, wet it, and scrubbed at my wrists and neck. When I couldn't smell the perfume anymore, I went back to Hunter's room. But before I even entered it, I could hear him sneezing.

"Ah-choo! Ah-choo! Look, here's the door to the space statiod, Bary Adde," he said when he saw me.

"Hunter, that's great, but . . . just a sec." I was looking around his room. What could be making him sneeze so much? I closed his windows. Then I closed his door. I laid my sweat shirt against the crack at the bottom of the door to keep dust from coming in. Then it occurred to me that maybe Hunter was allergic to my sweat shirt, so I opened the door and tossed it into the hallway. I thought for a few moments, then took off my socks and shoes and tossed *them* into the hallway. That ought to do it.

"Ah-choo! Ah-choo!"

Nope.

"Hunter," I said, "subthig, I mean something, is making you sneeze extra sneezes. I think maybe it's your erector set. You'd just gotten it out when you began sneezing. Maybe the pieces are dusty. Or maybe the box is dusty."

"Doe," said Hunter, and he grabbed for a tissue. "Do't bother puttig it away. Ah-choo! It's dot the erector set. I doe what's bakig be sdeeze. Ah-choo! Cub od. I'll show you."

Hunter led me into Kerry's room. What was he going to show me? A little dust bunny under her bed? No, he opened Kerry's closet. He motioned to me.

"Ah-ah-ah-ah-AH-AH-CHOOOO!" Hunter sneezed the biggest sneeze I've ever heard from a five-year-old. "Look id the box," he managed to say.

Then Hunter backed away and I stepped into the closet. On the floor was a large cardboard carton. I peered inside. Down at the bottom was . . . Tigger!

I gasped. "Tigger!" I cried. "Oh, *Tigger!*" I lifted him out of the box gently, as if he would break, and cradled him in my arms. Then I held him up to my face and felt the start of his Tigger-purr against my cheek. "Have you been here all along?" I whispered to him. I turned to Hunter. "Has he been here all this time?" But before Hunter could say a word, I turned back to Tigger, "Oh, I missed you *so* much. I really did. I thought you were, um," (I glanced at Hunter) "I thought you were . . . hurt. But, oh, it doesn't matter. I *missed* you!"

Tigger was nuzzling my arm, and I felt as if I never wanted to put him down, but then I noticed Hunter. He was sitting on Kerry's bed, sneezing practically nonstop, a raggedy tissue in his hands.

"Oops," I said. "Tigger, I *really* hate to do this, but I'm going to have to put you back in the box. Later this afternoon, though, you're going to come home with me."

"Is he *yours?*" asked Hunter as we left Kerry's room.

"Yes," I replied. For good measure, I closed her door behind us. Then I went to the bathroom and washed my hands and arms and face. I couldn't believe that I was abandoning Tigger, even if it was only temporarily, but he looked fine, and Hunter came first. After all, I was baby-sitting.

As you might imagine, I had an awful lot of questions. So I decided to talk to Hunter. The two of us sat at the kitchen table. (I thought the kitchen was probably the most dust-free room on the first floor.)

Hunter wasn't much help, though.

"How long have you known Tigger was here?" I asked him.

"Just sidce this bordig. I foud him by accidet. Kerry said dot to tell iddybody she has hib. She says they'll be bad because of by allergies. But I just had to tell subbody."

"You did the right thing," I told Hunter. "Does *any*one else know Tigger's here?"

Hunter shrugged. "Do't doe."

"How did Kerry get Tigger?"

"Do't doe."

"Did you know Tigger's *my* kitten?" I asked.

"Doe. Dot till you picked hib up ad everythig."

"Does Kerry know he's my kitten?"

Hunter shrugged again.

"Well, Logan certainly knows he's my kitten," I said.

"But I do't doe if Logad dows he's here."

"Oh. Right. . . . Hunter, you know I'll have to tell your mom about Tigger, don't you?" I added. "Even though Kerry might get in trouble."

Hunter nodded. "I doe." He looked worried and relieved at the same time.

It seemed like hours, of course, before the Brunos came home. That always happens when you're waiting desperately for something. But at last they arrived. And they were in pretty good moods. Nobody, it turned out, had had a single cavity, so they were going to celebrate.

But they were waiting for a day when Hunter was feeling better, and when Mr. Bruno could join them.

"How did everything go, Mary Anne?" Mrs. Bruno finally asked.

I couldn't see anything to do but to come right out with the truth. Hunter and I glanced at each other nervously. He knew what was coming.

"Mrs. Bruno," I began, and suddenly I found that I couldn't look at Logan. If he had known about Tigger all this time, then . . . then we couldn't be friends anymore. We just couldn't. "Mrs. Bruno, today Hunter couldn't stop sneezing, so I went looking for whatever was making him sneeze so much and — and there's a kitten in Kerry's closet!" This wasn't a lie, but it didn't point the finger at poor Hunter. He'd been right to show me Tigger, and I didn't want Kerry calling him a tattletale.

"A kitten!" cried Mrs. Bruno.

I finally glanced at Logan. He looked surprised. But was he surprised that a kitten had been found in Kerry's closet, or just surprised that Kerry had been found out?

"Yes," I said, "a kitten. And — and he's *my* kitten. He's been missing for five days. We've been searching for him everywhere."

"*Tigger* is in *Kerry's closet?*" Logan exclaimed.

All Mrs. Bruno could do was cry, "What?" and head for the stairs. Logan, Kerry, Hunter, and I followed her. When she reached Kerry's room, she flung open the door, raced for the closet, slid the box out, and exclaimed, "There *is* a kitten!"

"And it *is* Tigger," added Logan.

As if he didn't know, I thought.

Hunter began sneezing again, so Mrs. Bruno told him to go downstairs. Then she looked at Kerry. "Well," she said, "I think we have a little talking to do."

Kerry nodded miserably, her eyes on the ground. She sat on her bed and Mrs. Bruno sat next to her. Logan and I kind of stood around, unable to look at each other.

"How did you get Tigger?" Mrs. Bruno asked.

"I — I just found him," replied Kerry. "And I didn't know he was Tigger then. Honest. I was riding my bike home last Friday and it was getting dark. Remember? The weather wasn't very nice that day. And I was a few houses away from Mary Anne's and I thought I saw something shiny by the side of the road. So I stopped. And it was this kitten. Its eyes were shining. I thought, Poor kitty, no one's taking care of you. So I just put him in my bike basket and rode him home. I wanted to have a friend. And I wanted to show you and Daddy that I could care for a pet. I really am responsible enough to do that. Look how well I cared for Tigger."

Kerry jumped up. She began pulling things out of the closet. "See? With my own money I bought this food and this toy and these dishes and I never once forgot to feed Tigger. Or change his water. He's my friend."

Even I had to admit that Tigger looked well cared for.

"But honey," said Mrs. Bruno, "you know we can't have a cat, no matter how responsible you are. Hunter's just too allergic."

Kerry put Tigger's things back in the closet. Then she faced us, biting at one of her nails. "Um, I was also hoping to prove that Hunter would be okay as long as the cat stayed in my room. But — but I guess it didn't work."

Mrs. Bruno closed her eyes for a moment. When she opened them, she said, "Kerry, I'm a little confused. *Did* you know the kitten belonged to Mary Anne?"

"Not at first," said Kerry. "I really didn't. I thought he was lost or that somebody had dumped him by the side of the road. Then Logan told us about Tigger and I figured it out, only I thought, well, Mary Anne isn't taking very good care of him if she lets him wander away. I decided he'd be better off with me."

Mrs. Bruno didn't agree with that, of course, so she and Kerry kept talking. My mind began to wander. I thought of how different Logan had seemed lately, of how he'd sounded kind of irritated that us baby-sitters wanted him to come to our meetings about Tigger, and how he'd jumped right in and been so helpful when I got the ransom note. He must have known all along that Kerry had Tigger, so he was trying to protect her. The ransom note was perfect. Kerry hadn't sent it. Logan could help with the Tigger-napping all he wanted, look like a hero, and keep Kerry's secret.

I couldn't stand it any longer. "I have to go," I said huskily. I grabbed Tigger and headed down the hallway.

"But I haven't paid you yet!" Mrs. Bruno called after me.

"I'll get it tomorrow!" I shouted back.

Logan was at my heels. "Mary Anne, what's wrong?" he cried as I barged through the front door.

"You know what's wrong," I answered icily. "You knew about Tigger all along — and you didn't tell me."

I placed Tigger in the basket on my bicycle and sped down the Brunos' driveway, without giving Logan a chance to answer me.

CHAPTER 15

Wednesday afternoon — late.

Things happened fast. Everyone found out about Tigger quickly. (Of course, I made a lot of phone calls, carefully leaving out the part about Logan.) Then, instead of holding a club meeting, Claudia and Mallory and I walked through the neighborhood and took down as many of the Tigger posters as we could find. Dawn gave back everyone's portion of the reward money and returned the remainder to the treasury envelope. Later, I spent as much time with Tigger as possible — talking to him, cuddling him, playing with him. That night, he slept with me.

I did not let Tigger outside.

Thursday.

I did not talk to Logan. In school, we avoided each other. He sat with his guy friends at lunchtime.

"Is anything wrong between you and Logan?" Kristy asked me as we sat down in the cafeteria.

I nodded.

"But you don't want to talk about it?" said Dawn.

I shook my head. I didn't want to speak. I was afraid I'd cry. Logan and I had had fights before, but this one was different. I'd never accused him of anything so awful. And I'd never felt so unsure about us. If Logan could keep Tigger from me, what did that say about our relationship? By the end of the day, I just had to know.

I waited for Logan at his locker.

"Hi," he said shortly when he saw me.

"Hi," I replied. I stepped aside so he could work his combination lock.

When his locker was open, I said, "Can I talk to you?"

"Not now. I've got baseball practice."

"Later? I'm not baby-sitting this afternoon. I'll be at home."

"Will we have to sit outside?"

"Yup." (Logan knew that.)

He sighed.

"Come on. It's a beautiful day," I told him. "And I really do want to talk."

"Okay. I'll be there. See you later."

Logan closed his locker, turned, and strode down the hall.

Well, I thought, this is better than nothing.

I walked home with Claudia. When I reached my house, the first thing I did was pick up Tigger. "Oh, it's so nice to find you here when I get home from school," I told him. I lifted him up so we were eye to eye.

"Mrow?" asked Tigger.

"I don't know," I answered. "Logan's coming over this afternoon. He'll explain everything then, I hope."

I made sure that a bottle of Logan's favorite soda was in the refrigerator. I made sure we had ice cubes. Soda over ice in a glass is much nicer than warmish soda in a can.

At five o'clock, our bell rang. I ran to the front door and threw it open. Logan stood on our steps, mitt in one hand, books under one arm.

"Sit down," I told him. "I'll be right back. I'm getting you something to drink."

Actually, I was getting more than that. By the time Logan rang the bell, I'd fixed up a tray. I'd put a plate of cookies in the middle and next to it a couple of napkins. Now I set the glasses on it, added the ice and soda, and carried the tray to the front door, which I managed to open as I rested the tray against the wall. When the tray and I were safely outside, Logan looked at us in surprise.

"What's all this?" he asked.

"Nothing," I replied. (What a dumb answer. It was cookies and soda. And I'd fixed them because I hoped to make up with Logan.)

Logan took a soda and drank about half the glass in one gulp. How do boys do that? I mean, without exploding from the carbonation. Then he looked at me as if to say, "Well?"

I breathed in deeply, then exhaled. "Logan," I began, "just answer one question for me, okay?"

"Okay."

"Did you know that Kerry was hiding Tigger in her room?"

"No."

"Really?"

"That's two questions. And Mary Anne, I don't lie. To be honest, I'm really hurt that you could even think I'd do such a thing. *Why* would you think that, anyway?"

"Because . . . because . . ." Don't fall apart, I told myself. Sometimes when people accuse me of things, or sound like they're accusing me of things, I just crumple up and start to cry. So I took another deep breath (this is very relaxing, by the way) and said slowly, "Because of the way you've been acting lately. You snap at me, and you didn't seem to be very sympathetic when Tigger was missing. I know you helped with the search — the posters and everything — but it seemed like a huge chore for you. So I thought you knew about Kerry and Tigger and were just trying to protect Kerry. After all, she's your sister."

"And you're my Mary Anne." Logan polished off the cookie he'd been eating, and put his arm around me. "I could never hurt you. Not on purpose. I couldn't lie to you. Don't you know that?"

"I thought I did. But you *have* hurt me lately. You've changed."

Logan looked down at the grass. "You might as well know," he said. "I'm about to get kicked off the baseball team."

"You are? Why?" I couldn't believe it. Logan had been the star of his school team in Louisville.

"Coach doesn't like me. He expects more of me than of anyone else. And I start making stupid mistakes because of that."

"Oh." I remembered what Dawn had told me, how she'd watched Logan drop a ball that was right in his mitt.

"So a little while ago, Coach said I'd be off the team if I didn't improve. And I've been trying to improve. I really have. But Coach yells at me all the time and just makes me so nervous. I'm thinking of quitting before I get kicked off."

"Wow."

"Yeah. But I guess I kind of took my baseball problem out on you. That wasn't fair."

"It's okay. I should never have accused you of knowing about Tigger. That wasn't fair, either."

"Kerry is a champion sneak," added Logan. "She could hide a whale in the house and we'd never notice him."

"Not until you smelled him."

Logan and I laughed.

Then Logan said seriously, "I bet Kerry would change one hundred percent if she could just make some friends here."

"Well, I can help with that. I'll try to get her together with Becca Ramsey or Charlotte Johanssen."

"Hey, that'd be great! Listen, Mary Anne, I'm sorry about the way I acted."

"And I'm sorry about the things I said. . . . Is our fight over?"

"Yes. . . . Are the neighbors watching us?"

"Probably. That's the purpose of this outdoor arrangement."

Logan made a face. "Then let's just promise that from now on, we'll be more honest with each other."

"I promise," I said solemnly.

"Me, too," replied Logan.

Friday.

Club meeting day. At five-thirty we gathered in Claudia's room. Tigger was with me. He was curled up in my lap.

As soon as our opening business was taken care of, the phone rang.

"First job of the day!" said Kristy gaily, as she reached for the receiver. She picked it up. "Hello, Baby-sitters Club. . . . Oh, hi, Logan. Hold on. Here she is." Kristy handed me the phone, saying, "If it isn't a job offer, keep it short."

Ms. Bossy.

"Hi, Logan," I said. "What's up? *Oh* . . ."

I listened for quite awhile. When I'd hung up, I turned to the other girls. "It was a Kerry update," I said. "Logan thought you'd like to know what's happened, since you were all involved with the search for Tigger."

Five heads nodded.

"Okay. Well, of course Mr. and Mrs. Bruno were not too happy about what Kerry had done, but they understood *why* she'd done it.

She's going to be punished lightly, like, she has to wash the Brunos' cars or something, for keeping Tigger when she knew he belonged to me, and for bringing an animal into the house, especially so near to Hunter's room. However, the Brunos also think Kerry proved she's responsible enough to care for a pet. So tomorrow she and her parents will go to the pet store and Kerry will get to choose a hairless animal, like a turtle or some fish. Plus, next Wednesday, she's going over to Charlotte's house. She needs a friend her age. And one who's human."

"That's great!" cried Claud, and the others agreed.

The meeting continued. When the numbers on Claud's digital clock turned to 6:00, Kristy said, "Well, meeting's over."

Everyone stood up, except me.

"Come on, Mary Anne," called Dawn.

"Can't," I said. "Tigger's asleep."

Kristy groaned. "You are overprotecting that kitten."

"Yeah. You're treating him, oh, kind of the way your dad used to treat you," said Claud.

I stuck my tongue out at her and everyone laughed. Then I said, "All I know is that Tigger will not be allowed to start dating until he's at least sixteen. And I will never, ever let him get his driver's license. Or have his ears pierced."

"How about his nose?" asked Kristy, as I struggled to my feet.

I held the sleeping Tigger out toward her. "On *this* baby?"

Tigger opened his eyes sleepily and yawned in Kristy's face.

"Mmm. Cat-food breath," she said.

The six of us began giggling again as we headed downstairs.

Cat-food breath or not, I was thrilled to have Tigger back — and Logan, too.

Dear Reader:

I named Mary Anne's kitten after the first cat my family ever had. Before I was born, my parents lived in an apartment complex in Princeton, New Jersey. One day, one of the neighbors saw a young stray cat being attacked by a blue jay in the yard. The neighbor gave the cat to my parents, and they named him Tigger, after the tiger in *Winnie the Pooh*. Tigger lived to be seventeen years old and was one of our favorite pets, even though he remained shy and scared throughout his long life.

When I was young, my family had lots of cats. None of them was ever stolen, like Mary Anne's, but every now and then one would disappear for a day or two. We always worried, just like Mary Anne. Once, though, while we were on vacation, one of the cats escaped from the boarding kennel and found her way all across town to our house, even though she had never been outside our yard before. Just like in the book *The Incredible Journey*!

Happy reading,

Ann M Martin

L. GODWIN

Ann M. Martin

About the Author

ANN MATTHEWS MARTIN was born on August 12, 1955. She grew up in Princeton, NJ, with her parents and her younger sister, Jane.

Although Ann used to be a teacher and then an editor of children's books, she's now a full-time writer. She gets the ideas for her books from many different places. Some are based on personal experiences. Others are based on childhood memories and feelings. Many are written about contemporary problems or events.

All of Ann's characters, even the members of the Baby-sitters Club, are made up. (So is Stoneybrook.) But many of her characters are based on real people. Sometimes Ann names her characters after people she knows, other times she chooses names she likes.

In addition to the Baby-sitters Club books, Ann Martin has written many other books for children. Her favorite is *Ten Kids, No Pets* because she loves big families and she loves animals. Her favorite Baby-sitters Club book is *Kristy's Big Day*. (By the way, Kristy is her favorite baby-sitter!)

Ann M. Martin now lives in New York with her cats, Gussie and Woody. Her hobbies are reading, sewing, and needlework — especially making clothes for children.

The Baby-sitters Club

Notebook Pages

This Baby-sitters Club book belongs to _____.

I am _____ years old and in the _____

grade.

The name of my school is _____.

I got this BSC book from _____.

I started reading it on _____ and

finished reading it on _____.

The place where I read most of this book is _____.

My favorite part was when _____.

If I could change anything in the story, it might be the part when

_____.

My favorite character in the Baby-sitters Club is _____.

The BSC member I am most like is _____

because _____.

If I could write a Baby-sitters Club book it would be about ____

_____.

#25 Mary Anne and the Search for Tigger

Mary Anne is very scared when her cat Tigger is lost. One thing I'm very afraid of losing is _____ _____ . Whenever I lose something, the first place I look for it is _____ . The most important thing I ever lost was _____ _____ . One person I know who is always losing things is _____ . One person I know who is good at finding things is _____ . Dawn's mother is always finding her keys in the refrigerator and her shoes in the microwave. The strangest place I've ever found something was _____ . When Tigger is lost, Mary Anne and her friends must go on a big search. The biggest search I've ever been on was when I was looking for _____ _____ . If I ever had to search for something important, these are the people I would want searching with me: _____ _____ .

MARY ANNE'S

Party girl -- age 4

Sitting for the Pikes is always an adventure.

Sitting for Andrea and Jenny Prezzioso -- a quiet moment.

Logan and me.
Summer luv at Sea City.

Illustrations by Angelo Tillery

My family...
Jeff, Dad and Sharon
Dawn and me and Tigger.

Read all the books
about **Mary Anne**
in the Baby-sitters Club series
by Ann M. Martin

THE BABY-SITTERS CLUB®

Collect 'em all!

100 (and more)
Reasons to Stay Friends Forever!

❏ MG43388-1	#1	Kristy's Great Idea	$3.50
❏ MG43387-3	#10	Logan Likes Mary Anne!	$3.99
❏ MG43717-8	#15	Little Miss Stoneybrook...and Dawn	$3.50
❏ MG43722-4	#20	Kristy and the Walking Disaster	$3.50
❏ MG43347-4	#25	Mary Anne and the Search for Tigger	$3.50
❏ MG42498-X	#30	Mary Anne and the Great Romance	$3.50
❏ MG42508-0	#35	Stacey and the Mystery of Stoneybrook	$3.50
❏ MG44082-9	#40	Claudia and the Middle School Mystery	$3.25
❏ MG43574-4	#45	Kristy and the Baby Parade	$3.50
❏ MG44969-9	#50	Dawn's Big Date	$3.50
❏ MG44968-0	#51	Stacey's Ex-Best Friend	$3.50
❏ MG44966-4	#52	Mary Anne + 2 Many Babies	$3.50
❏ MG44967-2	#53	Kristy for President	$3.25
❏ MG44965-6	#54	Mallory and the Dream Horse	$3.25
❏ MG44964-8	#55	Jessi's Gold Medal	$3.25
❏ MG45657-1	#56	Keep Out, Claudia!	$3.50
❏ MG45658-X	#57	Dawn Saves the Planet	$3.50
❏ MG45659-8	#58	Stacey's Choice	$3.50
❏ MG45660-1	#59	Mallory Hates Boys (and Gym)	$3.50
❏ MG45662-8	#60	Mary Anne's Makeover	$3.50
❏ MG45663-6	#61	Jessi and the Awful Secret	$3.50
❏ MG45664-4	#62	Kristy and the Worst Kid Ever	$3.50
❏ MG45665-2	#63	Claudia's Special Friend	$3.50
❏ MG45666-0	#64	Dawn's Family Feud	$3.50
❏ MG45667-9	#65	Stacey's Big Crush	$3.50
❏ MG47004-3	#66	Maid Mary Anne	$3.50
❏ MG47005-1	#67	Dawn's Big Move	$3.50
❏ MG47006-X	#68	Jessi and the Bad Baby-sitter	$3.50
❏ MG47007-8	#69	Get Well Soon, Mallory!	$3.50
❏ MG47008-6	#70	Stacey and the Cheerleaders	$3.50
❏ MG47009-4	#71	Claudia and the Perfect Boy	$3.99
❏ MG47010-8	#72	Dawn and the We Love Kids Club	$3.99
❏ MG47011-6	#73	Mary Anne and Miss Priss	$3.99
❏ MG47012-4	#74	Kristy and the Copycat	$3.99
❏ MG47013-2	#75	Jessi's Horrible Prank	$3.50
❏ MG47014-0	#76	Stacey's Lie	$3.50
❏ MG48221-1	#77	Dawn and Whitney, Friends Forever	$3.99
❏ MG48222-X	#78	Claudia and Crazy Peaches	$3.50
❏ MG48223-8	#79	Mary Anne Breaks the Rules	$3.50
❏ MG48224-6	#80	Mallory Pike, #1 Fan	$3.99

More titles... ▶

❏ MG48225-4	#81	Kristy and Mr. Mom	$3.50
❏ MG48226-2	#82	Jessi and the Troublemaker	$3.99
❏ MG48235-1	#83	Stacey vs. the BSC	$3.50
❏ MG48228-9	#84	Dawn and the School Spirit War	$3.50
❏ MG48236-X	#85	Claudi Kishi, Live from WSTO	$3.50
❏ MG48227-0	#86	Mary Anne and Camp BSC	$3.50
❏ MG48237-8	#87	Stacey and the Bad Girls	$3.50
❏ MG22872-2	#88	Farewell, Dawn	$3.50
❏ MG22873-0	#89	Kristy and the Dirty Diapers	$3.50
❏ MG22874-9	#90	Welcome to the BSC, Abby	$3.50
❏ MG22875-1	#91	Claudia and the First Thanksgiving	$3.50
❏ MG22876-5	#92	Mallory's Christmas Wish	$3.50
❏ MG22877-3	#93	Mary Anne and the Memory Garden	$3.99
❏ MG22878-1	#94	Stacey McGill, Super Sitter	$3.99
❏ MG22879-X	#95	Kristy + Bart = ?	$3.99
❏ MG22880-3	#96	Abby's Lucky Thirteen	$3.99
❏ MG22881-1	#97	Claudia and the World's Cutest Baby	$3.99
❏ MG22882-X	#98	Dawn and Too Many Baby-sitters	$3.99
❏ MG69205-4	#99	Stacey's Broken Heart	$3.99
❏ MG69206-2	#100	Kristy's Worst Idea	$3.99
❏ MG45575-3		Logan's Story Special Edition Readers' Request	$3.25
❏ MG47118-X		Logan Bruno, Boy Baby-sitter	
		Special Edition Readers' Request	$3.50
❏ MG47756-0		Shannon's Story Special Edition	$3.50
❏ MG47686-6		The Baby-sitters Club Guide to Baby-sitting	$3.25
❏ MG47314-X		The Baby-sitters Club Trivia and Puzzle Fun Book	$2.50
❏ MG48400-1		BSC Portrait Collection: Claudia's Book	$3.50
❏ MG22864-1		BSC Portrait Collection: Dawn's Book	$3.50
❏ MG69181-3		BSC Portrait Collection: Kristy's Book	$3.99
❏ MG22865-X		BSC Portrait Collection: Mary Anne's Book	$3.99
❏ MG48399-4		BSC Portrait Collection: Stacey's Book	$3.50
❏ MG92713-2		The Complete Guide to the Baby-sitters Club	$4.95
❏ MG47151-1		The Baby-sitters Club Chain Letter	$14.95
❏ MG48295-5		The Baby-sitters Club Secret Santa	$14.95
❏ MG45074-3		The Baby-sitters Club Notebook	$2.50
❏ MG44783-1		The Baby-sitters Club Postcard Book	$4.95

Available wherever you buy books...or use this order form.
Scholastic Inc., P.O. Box 7502, 2931 E. McCarty Street, Jefferson City, MO 65102

Please send me the books I have checked above. I am enclosing $_____
(please add $2.00 to cover shipping and handling). Send check or money order—
no cash or C.O.D.s please.

Name_____ Birthdate_____

Address _____

City_____ State/Zip _____

BSC596

THE BABY-SITTERS CLUB®

by Ann M. Martin

Collect and read these exciting BSC Super Specials, Mysteries, and Super Mysteries along with your favorite Baby-sitters Club books!

BSC Super Specials

❑ BBK44240-6	Baby-sitters on Board! Super Special #1	$3.95
❑ BBK44239-2	Baby-sitters' Summer Vacation Super Special #2	$3.95
❑ BBK43973-1	Baby-sitters' Winter Vacation Super Special #3	$3.95
❑ BBK42493-9	Baby-sitters' Island Adventure Super Special #4	$3.95
❑ BBK43575-2	California Girls! Super Special #5	$3.95
❑ BBK43576-0	New York, New York! Super Special #6	$4.50
❑ BBK44963-X	Snowbound! Super Special #7	$3.95
❑ BBK44962-X	Baby-sitters at Shadow Lake Super Special #8	$3.95
❑ BBK45661-X	Starring The Baby-sitters Club! Super Special #9	$3.95
❑ BBK45674-1	Sea City, Here We Come! Super Special #10	$3.95
❑ BBK47015-9	The Baby-sitters Remember Super Special #11	$3.95
❑ BBK48308-0	Here Come the Bridesmaids! Super Special #12	$3.95
❑ BBK22883-8	Aloha, Baby-sitters! Super Special #13	$4.50

BSC Mysteries

❑ BAI44084-5	#1	Stacey and the Missing Ring	$3.50
❑ BAI44085-3	#2	Beware Dawn!	$3.50
❑ BAI44799-8	#3	Mallory and the Ghost Cat	$3.50
❑ BAI44800-5	#4	Kristy and the Missing Child	$3.50
❑ BAI44801-3	#5	Mary Anne and the Secret in the Attic	$3.50
❑ BAI44961-3	#6	The Mystery at Claudia's House	$3.50
❑ BAI44960-5	#7	Dawn and the Disappearing Dogs	$3.50
❑ BAI44959-1	#8	Jessi and the Jewel Thieves	$3.50
❑ BAI44958-3	#9	Kristy and the Haunted Mansion	$3.50
❑ BAI45696-2	#10	Stacey and the Mystery Money	$3.50

More titles ➡

The Baby-sitters Club books continued...

THE BABY-SITTERS CLUB®

Meet the best friends you'll ever have!

by Ann M. Martin

ALL NEW!

Have you heard? The BSC has a new look
—and more great stuff than ever before.
An all-new scrapbook for each book's narrator!
A letter from Ann M. Martin! Fill-in pages to
personalize your copy! Order today!

❏ BBD22473-5	#1	**Kristy's Great Idea**		$3.50
❏ BBD22763-7	#2	**Claudia and the Phantom Phone Calls**		$3.99
❏ BBD25158-9	#3	**The Truth About Stacey**		$3.99
❏ BBD25159-7	#4	**Mary Anne Saves the Day**		$3.50
❏ BBD25160-0	#5	**Dawn and the Impossible Three**		$3.50
❏ BBD25161-9	#6	**Kristy's Big Day**		$3.50
❏ BBD25162-7	#7	**Claudia and Mean Janine**		$3.50
❏ BBD25163-5	#8	**Boy Crazy Stacey**		$3.50
❏ BBD25164-3	#9	**The Ghost at Dawn's House**		$3.99
❏ BBD25165-1	#10	**Logan Likes Mary Anne!**		$3.99
❏ BBD25166-X	#11	**Kristy and the Snobs**		$3.99
❏ BBD25167-8	#12	**Claudia and the New Girl**		$3.99

Available wherever you buy books, or use this order form.

■ SCHOLASTIC